STAKES & SPURS

VENOM VALLEY

BOOK TWO

HANK EDWARDS

MITTEN GINGER MEDIA

SUMMARY

New lovers torn apart.
An ancient evil consuming a small town.
Unlikely heroes running out of time.

Dex Wells, former deputy of the prairie town of Belkin's Pass, has been taken captive by the wicked vampire Balthazar and held in the caves above Venom Valley. He knows he is being kept as bait, a way to lure Dex's lover, Josh, into the caves in order to capture him. As Dex tries to escape, he realizes he's not the only prisoner Balthazar keeps chained in those dark depths.

Josh Stanton can raise the dead. It's a power he's always had within him but never understood. Now, he's trying to become more skilled at wielding that power, and using it to battle Balthazar and rescue Dex. But there's still a bounty on Josh's head for a murder he did not commit, and he ends up back in Belkin's Pass with Glory, a half White, half Apache former saloon girl watched over by a Native American spirit.

Two members of the US Army arrive and, with no lawmen left in town, take Josh into custody. It's up to Josh and Glory to convince these men the truth about their small town and find a way to save Dex before Balthazar turns him into a vampire as well.

CONTENTS

CHAPTER

ONE

D ex woke to screaming.

He lay on a stone floor. Gritty dirt crunched beneath his skull as he rolled his head back and forth. A chill had worked its way through him, into him, and made him shiver.

The screaming continued. It was a woman, her voice high pitched, tinged with desperate madness.

His eyes fluttered open to darkness. A cold knot of fear tightened in his chest.

I've lost my sight, he thought.

He sat up and started at the clank and feel of chains around his wrists.

"Josh?" he said into the darkness. His voice echoed back to him, and the screams stopped. The sudden silence was more unsettling than the screaming.

But it lasted only a moment, no longer than a breath, and then the woman resumed. It wasn't a scream of fear, however. No panic or terror iced the sound, but that somehow made it even more frightening.

Where was he?

He waved a hand before his eyes, relieved that he was able to see its pale outline. He wasn't blind after all, just somewhere dark. Very dark. And he was chained. Thick metal cuffs bound his wrists, attached to heavy links that snaked away into the darkness.

Dex slid across the cold floor, following the chains to a stone wall. He traced the links up the wall and found that what he thought were two chains was actually one length looped through a metal ring in the wall. He grabbed the chain to either side of the ring and pulled, but the ring was bolted fast to the stone.

With a shout of frustration and fear that momentarily drowned out the screams of the unseen woman, he gave up and dropped to the floor. Sitting with his back against the stone wall, he closed his eyes. He took a deep breath, gathered his strength, and shouted as loud as he could, "Josh!"

His voice echoed back to him, and the woman fell silent again.

Moments later, she screamed, "Josh!" A trembling, high-pitched laugh followed, the sound of it sending shivers through Dex, and he decided it might be best to remain silent.

The woman started her ranting scream again, but Dex tried to block out the sound by thinking back to his last memory. He had been with Josh in the Indian teepee, kissing him, loving him, finally feeling safe after Glory and the tribe had rescued them from the undead miners. He remembered noticing the camp outside the teepee had gone quiet, and he and Josh had gotten dressed then stepped out of the shelter into the firelight. But what had happened after that?

He closed his eyes against the dark, squeezed them shut

tight, and thought back. Josh's face floated into his mind, and a twinge of lonely longing rippled through him, leaving an empty ache in its wake. He wanted to be with Josh, hold him, and be able to turn his head and see Josh beside him, know he was safe.

The screams echoed around him. The woman nearby had started up again and her piercing voice tore his thoughts to shreds. He raised his hands, the chains rattling and clanging, and grabbed fistfuls of his hair.

"Quiet! Please!" Dex called.

The screams trailed off, leaving him surrounded by silence in the forsaken darkness.

Dex drew in a breath and thought back again. Josh. The teepee. The tribe that had rescued them, cared for Josh, clothed and fed them. Something had happened at the camp. Something or someone had come...

Screams again, ripping into his mind, pulling him out of his thoughts and back to the cold stone walls of the cave.

"Dammit," Dex whispered. "What happened to me?"

He struggled to his feet, his body stiff from the hard stone floor. His limbs ached, and he needed to move. He paced to the full reach of the chains then turned to pace back until he reached the wall. At one point he turned and became tangled in the chains. Dex lifted his arms, and the cold, greasy links draped across his throat. The feeling brought back a memory, the touch of a cold, strong hand on his throat, the sight of Josh standing a distance away, staring at him.

Whose hand had been at his throat?

The shrieks slowed, and then started up again, shattering his concentration, and he pressed his back to the stone wall, put his face in his hands, and slid to the floor.

"Josh…," Dex whispered. "Where are you?"

"Josh is quite far away."

The voice came from the darkness right in front of him, and Dex let out a startled bark of surprise.

"Oh," the voice cooed. "Did I scare you? Many apologies. I forget, sometimes, how dark it is in here. A moment, if you will."

The flare of the match felt like the sun at high noon to Dex's light-starved eyes. He turned away, blinking until his eyes had adjusted. When he looked back, he saw a tall, broad shouldered man with dark hair and a pale complexion standing in the yellow glow of a candle. He was handsome and narrow-waisted, the black shirt and trousers he wore well-tailored to his body. Shadows cloaked his deep-set eyes that seemed to glow red. Sharp fangs glittered in the candle-light when the man smiled, and an uneasy chill trembled up Dex's spine.

"Good evening," the man said.

Dex pushed up the wall to his feet, the chains rattling and slapping against his legs. "Who are you?" Then a name slammed into his mind and Dex blurted it as a cold knot of terror tightened in his gut. "Balthazar."

Balthazar bowed slightly at the waist. "Ah, my reputation precedes me. And you are deputy Dexter Wells, yes?"

"How do you know that?"

"I know many things, deputy." Balthazar suddenly stood very close beside him, and Dex jumped away, his heart pounding.

"How… how did you do that?" Dex asked.

"I can do many things." Balthazar leaned in closer. "So many things. I have had lifetimes to learn and listen."

Dex slid along the wall, putting distance between himself and Balthazar. "Stay away from me."

"Oh, come now, that's no way to treat a new acquaintance. But, since you are my guest, I shall respect your wishes." Balthazar walked off a few paces, and then turned back. "Does this suit you?"

Dex swallowed past the hard lump of fear lodged in his throat. "Better."

"Very good. Now, let's talk about Josh."

"Josh?" Dex pressed his palms against the rocky wall behind him in an effort to steady himself. "Leave him be. He's been through enough."

"Oh, but I think there's more he needs to go through. There's something special inside Josh. I sense something that makes him stand out from any others I have... encountered." Balthazar took two steps closer. "You are close to him, closer than any other, I could see that by his reaction at the camp. What do you know about Josh, Dex? What is it that churns inside him? Tell me, Dexter Wells. I would never betray a confidence and tell where I heard it. Just whisper it in my ear." Balthazar moved fast, suddenly standing right in front of him. He leaned in close, his face right next to Dex's, giving off waves of cold.

"I don't know what you're talking about," Dex said. His breath came in short, quick pants, and spots swarmed before his eyes. His thoughts were a scattered mess, as if they were made of glass and he had dropped them on the rocky floor. "Josh is just a man."

Balthazar drew back and caught Dex's gaze with his glowing red eyes. Warmth crept into Dex, stilling the biting cold of his terror as Balthazar said, "So valiant. But I will find out the truth about Josh. We have all the time in the world to talk. Well, I do."

Dex shook his head but felt his resolve weaken as he stared into Balthazar's eyes. He closed off thoughts of Josh and forced them into a far corner of his mind. "No matter what you do, there's nothing I can tell you."

Balthazar smiled. "I like you, Dex. You are loyal, and quite handsome. I think you would make a perfect partner to live out eternity with. Think of the power we would wield; the power that you could command. You would be able to bring so many to justice. Would that not be nice?"

"I'm not like you," Dex said.

"Oh, but you could be," Balthazar whispered. "Now, let us discuss your future, shall we?" Balthazar smiled, the sharp points of his teeth just visible behind his lips. "As short or long as that may be."

Dex's breath caught on the dread spreading through his chest. He closed his eyes and thought about Josh, picturing him safe and warm and happy. The image in his mind helped give him strength to straighten his posture. If he could just keep Balthazar from going after Josh, as long as he knew Josh was safe from Balthazar, Dex thought he could withstand anything that was done to him.

A slender trail of warmth worked through him, like the tiny sprouts of corn he had nurtured working in his family's fields. For a moment, just the flicker of a single breath, Dex felt as if he were with Josh. He felt his body heat, the movement of his arms and hips. In that moment, Dex could feel himself on horseback, seated behind Josh, his arms loosely draped around his hips, hands resting with comfortable familiarity on the tops of his thighs. He could almost smell his familiar scent.

The cold touch of Balthazar's fingers brought Dex out of that moment, and he gasped in fright. Any connection he might have had with Josh closed down, and somewhere inside, Dex believed he had, indeed been with Josh. He opened his eyes to find himself looking into Balthazar's smooth, handsome face. Balthazar held Dex's right arm in his hands, his grip tight and cold.

"It amazes me how fragile the body truly is," Balthazar said. He tightened his fingers into Dex's flesh, pressing the muscle beneath hard against the bone. "The skin, so thin, barely holding in all the blood, just managing to keep the wet mess of organs packed tight inside. Strip away the skin—" Balthazar ran the long, pointed tip of a fingernail down the length of Dex's forearm, drawing blood "—and all you're left with is ropes of muscle and sinew wrapped around solid bone."

Dex pulled in a breath and heard it hiss between his teeth as the warm trickle of blood ran along his arm. Balthazar held him fast, preventing Dex from pulling away.

"But even bone, the hardened frame of the body, is delicate in its way." Balthazar's fingers tightened even more around Dex's arm as blood dripped from between his fingers to the stone floor. "It breaks so easily when enough pressure is applied."

Pain swarmed Dex's reasoning. He tried to pull away, tried to get free, but Balthazar held him fast. His arm throbbed as muscle scraped harder over bone. He heard his screams echoed back to him from the woman held somewhere else in the cave. Balthazar smiled as he gripped Dex's arm, his lips parted enough to show the sharp points of his teeth.

Through the pain, memories spun into Dex's mind. He

had seen others with fangs like that, women from the saloon in town. He had fought them. He and Josh both had fought them.

But Josh wasn't with him now. Dex was alone with Balthazar, who was about to shatter his forearm and most likely drain the blood from his body. Dex would die here in this cave, and his body would rot and crumble into dust. No one he loved would find him and lay him to rest in hallowed ground. He was alone, and he was doomed.

The screaming woman matched his screams, their voices combining, blending into one long terrified wail. And then, just as Dex was certain he could take no more, that the pain and fear would push him over the brink of sanity... it got worse.

Balthazar lowered his mouth to the cut on his forearm. Dex felt the cold touch of his tongue against the warmth of his blood. He heard the slurp of Balthazar drinking his blood. As he drank, Balthazar twisted his hands around Dex's arm as if wringing the blood from him.

Dex's scream grew even louder, fading into the background of the sensation of Balthazar drinking from him. He put his head back, closed his eyes, and his thoughts drifted to Josh. He pictured Josh's face, the rounded jut of his chin, his dark blond hair and brown eyes. With thoughts of Josh fixed firmly in his mind, Dex felt a trickle of calm eke through the panicked fear. He longed for the feeling of riding behind Josh, wanted to feel the warmth of Josh's back against his chest, feel Josh's strong thighs beneath his hands. But his thoughts were too scattered by terror; all he could do was hope the end came fast.

Suddenly, Balthazar released him. Dex pulled his arm free, clutched it against his chest, and felt the warm gush of blood drench his shirt as he staggered back from Balthazar. He risked a glance over his shoulder as he walked unsteadily along the wall, sure he would see Balthazar right behind him, reaching out for him. But he was not there. Dex came to a stop, his throat raw from the force of his screams, his breathing short and fast. He looked around the cave, his gaze jumping from one spot to the next, trying to see all places and into all shadows at once.

"Did I frighten you?"

Dex jumped and cowered back from where Balthazar suddenly appeared beside the guttering candle. "My apologies. But, you see, I just had to sample your blood. It wasn't a bite, you see, just a scratch, yes? Think about how that felt, Dex, that tiny scratch. Think of all the scratches I could give you, all over your body, and how long it would take for you to die from those tiny scratches. Think about those things, and then consider whether or not Josh's secrets are worth all that." Balthazar smiled and reached over to pinch out the candle flame, allowing the unrelenting dark to surround Dex once again. "By the way, you were delicious."

The woman's screaming resumed, digging through the dark to surround Dex with fear.

Dex slid down the wall and held his bleeding arm tight against his chest. He drew in a few shaky breaths until his heart had slowed, then he closed his eyes and whispered into the darkness, "Josh."

TWO

Lightning split the heavy clouds and thunder followed immediately after. It rumbled through Josh's chest and spooked his horse. Clementine reared up as another jagged bolt of lightning lit the storm-darkened landscape.

And revealed the pack of wolves lurking not far behind.

"Easy girl," Josh shouted over the wind that slanted rain hard into his face. "Settle on down now."

"Josh!"

He turned to look over his shoulder. Glory sat astride Dex's horse, Nightshade.

Dex.

A quick flash of brilliant pain went through him.

"Look out!"

Glory's panicked voice cut through the storm, his fog of exhaustion, and the pain of watching Dex taken away. He clutched the reins just in time to keep from being thrown by Clementine as the horse dodged a skinny wolf that had crept close to nip at her flank. Clementine's rear hoof struck the wolf in the side and sent the animal yelping back toward its pack.

They moved the horses close together, facing opposite directions. Josh pulled out the revolver that Dex had left behind in the teepee, and Glory loaded a shell in her rifle.

"They're getting brave," Glory said.

"Desperate," Josh agreed.

The wolves surged forward as one. Their wet fur looked slick and matted in the lightning flashes as they surrounded the horses. Josh carefully fired the precious bullets, feeling a grim satisfaction as he watched four wolves drop dead to the ground. Until the revolver clicked on an empty chamber. "I'm out!" he shouted to Glory as he fumbled at the saddlebag for more ammunition.

She used the rifle sparingly, picking her targets, but the storm was throwing off her aim.

It was Dex's rifle she held, and though Josh tried to focus on reloading his pistol, his thoughts strayed to Dex, wondering where and how he was. He felt sure Dex was still alive, though he wasn't sure why. He could feel Dex sometimes, like a reassuring presence, so he had to believe Dex still lived.

Then, he felt a heat through the cold of the pouring rain and the bite of the wind through his wet clothing. It was as if someone sat on Clementine behind him, arms around his waist, hands resting on his thighs. The feeling was so strong, Josh paused with a bullet held between two fingers, ready to drop into the chamber.

"Dex," Josh whispered.

Lightning scorched the sky, followed quickly by a loud clap of thunder that made him jump.

"Josh!" Glory screamed.

Something grabbed his boot, tugged his foot out of the stirrup and pulled his leg taut. Josh dropped the bullet and barely managed to keep hold of the pistol. He grabbed the saddle horn and saved himself from falling into the mud. He felt teeth pierce the thick leather of his boot and scrape against the side of his foot.

Josh tried to kick his foot free, but the wolf's fangs were in too deep. Clementine snorted and rose up on her back legs, front hooves pawing at the clouds. The wolf held tight, pulling hard, and Josh felt himself slip sideways in the saddle.

"Glory!" he shouted.

She turned, brought up the rifle, and paused long enough for Josh to consider what she was about to do. If she missed, she could shatter his leg or cripple his horse. Cold rain ran down the back of his shirt as the wolf jerked his foot again.

Glory fired.

The wolf jumped and sagged, dead weight now, its fangs still hooked into Josh's boot.

"Dammit," Josh said as he kicked his leg. His knee ached with the effort to lift and shake his leg as the wolf's weight clung to him.

Finally, the drag on his leg let up, but at the cost of his boot. It slid off his foot and fell into the mud, still clutched in the wolf's mouth.

Josh was glad he'd worn socks as he slid his foot back into the stirrup and turned Clementine to face the nearest wolf. He still needed to finish reloading his pistol, and he tried to keep an eye on the wolves as he reached for more bullets.

"Behind us!" Glory shouted.

"I need to reload!" Josh responded, turning to look over his shoulder.

Another wolf charged them, fur rippling in the rain and wind.

A gunshot cracked from his left, and the wolf dropped into the mud. The sound brought them both around to look back the way they had come. Hope rose in Josh's chest as he squinted into the gray morning light, expecting to see members of the Indian tribe who had rescued him and Dex from the risen dead miners. His hope died, however, at the sight of two white men riding toward them. More gunshots scattered the remaining wolves.

"Who are they?" Glory asked.

"Trouble. Ride!" Josh shouted, and he dug his heels into Clementine's sides.

They rode beneath the storm clouds, the horses losing traction as they circled rocky outcrops and waded through flooded areas. Josh's bootless foot grew numb in the cold rain and wind. He had no idea where they were riding to; he just knew he needed to get away from the men behind them. A series of rock formations came up, and he pulled Clementine into the narrow passage between two of them, hoping to provide cover so they could lose their pursuers. He felt the horse's hooves slip on the wet surface of the rocky floor, and realized too late this might have been a bad idea.

"Josh!" Glory shouted over the wind and rain.

Josh looked over his shoulder. She hunched forward over Nightshade, hands gripping the reins, hair plastered to her head. Right behind her rode one of the men, hat pulled down tight on his head.

Just as he wondered where the second man had gone, a gunshot from in front of him brought him around. A man astride a horse waited at the opening of the passage, his rifle aimed right at Josh. He reined in Clementine and tried to think of what he could say to these men to talk himself free. He had a bounty on his head, but maybe these men didn't know about it. If they were robbers, they would be able to see they had nothing of value on them and would most likely let them go.

Unless they wanted to take their turns with Glory.

A flash of lightning revealed the man's face, and one fear replaced another.

Sheriff Haden sat tall in his saddle, rifle aimed right at Josh's chest, and eyes cold beneath the brim of his hat.

"Hand over the gun, Stanton," Haden ordered.

"Sheriff," Josh said, "you don't know what's going on."

"I know enough to arrest you for the murder of Agnes Pritchett, the woman who raised you as her own," Haden said. "Now hand over the gun."

Josh hesitated long enough for Haden to cock the rifle. The rock walls on either side hemmed them in, and when Josh looked over his shoulder, he saw that Wallace Underwood, the other deputy in Belkin's Pass, blocked the way they had come.

He looked back at Sheriff Haden and, from the look in the man's eyes, Josh realized Haden would shoot them both in the back without a second thought if they tried to run. Josh let out a shaky breath and turned to nod to Glory.

She frowned at him. "What about Dex?"

"We'll get there," Josh said through gritted teeth. "Just not today."

Wallace Underwood dismounted and slowly approached them. He grabbed Glory's rifle, then walked up to Josh and took his gun as well.

"Sheriff," Josh tried again, "we're heading toward the cliffs. Dex is in trouble and needs our help."

"Dexter Wells is no longer a deputy of Belkin's Pass," Haden stated in a flat, cold voice. "I didn't come out here for him or for you. I had written you both off to the vultures. But I must admit that finding you gives me some pleasure, despite my losses."

"Losses?" Glory asked.

Haden's eyes sharpened, and his lips pressed together. "None of your goddamn concern. Hold your hands out, wrists tight together. Wallace, tie them to the saddle horns. We'll take them back into town and gather more men to look for Hattie."

Josh turned away from watching Wallace tie his wrists. "Your daughter?"

"She's missing," Wallace said as he focused on tying a good knot. "Taken off in the night."

"Vampires," Glory whispered from over Josh's shoulder.

"Shut your damn mouths!" Haden shouted. "You too, deputy. These criminals don't need to know my business."

"Sorry, Sheriff," Wallace said.

Minutes later, Josh and Glory were tied tight, and their horses were being led back toward town. Josh tried to wriggle his hands free of the ropes, but there was no play. Despite his lack of intelligence, Wallace Underwood could tie a good knot, dammit.

"How long has Hattie been gone?" Josh called.

Haden ignored him, but Josh saw the man's shoulders tighten, lifting higher beneath his leather duster.

"There could still be a chance to save her," Glory shouted over the wind and rain. "She won't be turned for three nights."

Their only acknowledgement came from the rumble of thunder in the clouds above. Josh gave up any attempt at conversation and let himself drift as he sat tied to his saddle. He closed his eyes and thought about Dex to calm himself. He remembered the press of Dex's lips, the taste of his skin, the feel of Dex's cock, hard and strong in his fist. Josh could almost taste the salt of Dex's skin as the man's cock lay along his tongue. He could feel the hot sting of invasion as Dex filled him, completed him, pushed into him over and over until Dex had groaned and released his seed deep inside Josh.

A rumble of thunder startled him, and he opened his eyes, surprised to find they were only a few miles outside the town limits. He must have fallen asleep for a while and dreamed of Dex. Had he and Glory really been this close to Belkin's Pass? They must have gotten turned around in the storm.

Josh yawned and looked over at Glory, not surprised to find she too had drifted off to sleep. Neither of them had slept much the last two nights; they had taken turns keeping watch. Oddly, no vampires had approached them, only the wolves. He had expected an attack, and the fact that there had been no sign of Balthazar or any of his kind had made Josh more nervous than if they had appeared.

The rain had not let up, and he was soaked through, cold to the bone, which made the first flush of heat inside of him that much more noticeable. It started in the middle of his torso and slowly spread through him the closer they rode toward town. As the heat slid through his veins and dug into his limbs and organs, Josh swallowed past the fear in his throat and looked at his surroundings, because he knew what the sensation meant.

Death was close.

Staggered towers of rock gleamed dark in a flash of lightning, and he realized with a start the route Haden had taken to get back to town so fast. It was passable but seldom used by travelers due to the rugged terrain.

And it would take them right past the Belkin's Pass cemetery.

Josh closed his eyes and focused his energy and attention away from the bodies buried ahead. He was tired, though, and could feel them lying there, starving and cold. He could almost smell the damp earth pressing in around them, feel the cold in their bloodless limbs, the hunger for flesh should they awaken.

He needed to learn how to control this power, harness it, and use it only in extreme situations. Raising the dead was a sacrilege, an affront to the natural law of life and death. He needed to understand it, work through this power, and use it to keep the dead in their graves and not lurching toward people, hungry for blood. The power ran deep inside him, though, and he didn't have a firm grasp on it. Not yet. And especially not this exhausted. If he got near a body, it would rise and attack him and anyone with him, hungry for flesh, for life.

"Dark's comin' fast."

Glory's voice brought him out of his thoughts, and he looked at the sky swollen with thunderheads. She was right. The sun, hidden by heavy thunderheads, would almost be down.

"Shut up back there," Deputy Wallace snapped.

"We need to get inside," Josh called up to the men. "It's not safe out here after dark."

"I wouldn't think you'd be so eager to be inside," Sheriff Haden said over his shoulder, "seeing as how you'll be spending a long time inside a jail cell."

"The men who took your daughter will return when the sun goes down," Glory said. "They'll take anyone they find on the street or anyone who invites them into their homes. No one in town is safe anymore, don't you see?"

Haden reined in his horse and turned in the saddle. A quick movement brought his gun up, and Josh found himself impressed with the swiftness of the man's draw even as a tremor of fear worked through him. He never knew the sheriff was so adept with his weapon.

"You're not to speak about my daughter!" Haden shouted. "Not a word about my Hattie should come from your dirty whore mouth, do you understand?"

Josh looked over at Glory, watched her jaw tighten, and saw her sit up high and straight in the saddle. The muted final rays of light behind the storm clouds glittered in her dark eyes. Just when he thought she might say something to encourage Haden to shoot her, Glory surprised him by giving the man a single nod.

Relief unwound within Josh's gut, and he looked back at the sheriff, continuing to slowly work his wrists within the wet and loosening ropes.

"What in God's name...?"

Haden stared between Glory and Josh, to a spot somewhere behind them, and his expression changed from anger to confusion, and then to fear. Josh looked over his shoulder.

In a flash of lightning, he saw a number of figures striding toward them through the rain, a line of wolves following just behind.

"Vampires," Glory said.

THREE

Glory met Josh's eyes and saw her terror reflected back. "Untie us!" Josh shouted.

Sheriff Haden ignored him and called to the line of men and women that approached. "Stand where you are! As sheriff of Belkin's Pass, I order you to halt."

Glory pulled and twisted her hands within the bindings, the ropes biting into her skin, leaving raw red welts. "Set us free!"

"Sheriff, they ain't gonna stop," Wallace said with a tremor in his voice. "Is that Holden Olsen out there? He went missing days ago."

Haden fired off a shot, and Glory and Josh both jumped. She saw Josh pull hard against the ropes and his left hand slipped free, dark and slick with blood from his struggles. He disentangled his right hand, then loosened the rope from around his saddle horn, freeing Clementine from the sheriff's horse.

"Hey!" Wallace said, Josh's actions pulling his small eyes

from the approaching threat. "Stanton's loose! Hold it right—"

A dark shape flashed past Glory, and she felt the warmth of Ohanzee's protection surge into life, could almost feel his arms wrap around her. She cried out as she watched Wallace knocked to the ground. The sheriff started in his saddle and stared down to where the deputy kicked and screamed on the ground, his mouth working but no sound coming out. A woman held Wallace pinned to the muddy ground with one hand on his chest. She raised her face to the stormy sky, a flash of lightning gleaming off her fangs, and Glory saw a young Chinese girl whose name she thought was Ling. A shriek tore from Ling's throat, violent and hungry, and then she dropped her mouth to Wallace's throat.

"Let go of him!" Haden fired point blank into Ling's back, but the girl didn't even flinch. As Josh leaned over to help Glory with her bindings, another flash of lightning allowed her to see the fabric of Ling's dress flutter with each shot until the sheriff's revolver clicked on empty chambers.

"Hurry," Glory whispered. "They're coming."

"I'm trying."

"Use your knife!" she snapped.

Josh cursed and reached into the saddlebag to grab his Bowie knife. He freed Glory, and then loosed Nightshade from the deputy's horse. They each dug in their heels, and the horses raced through the dark rain toward town.

"Ride, Sheriff!" Josh called out as he and Glory passed to either side of the man.

Glory crouched low over the saddle, Ohanzee's presence fading as they left the danger behind. The wrought iron fences of the cemetery gleamed in the lightning like the spears of an undead army, and Glory glanced over at Josh.

His eyes were closed and his jaw clenched. She figured he was fighting back whatever power lived within him that brought back the dead. From the top of the cliff above the mine, Glory had witnessed the risen dead miners attacking the wolves and then Dex and Josh themselves. Once back at camp, Dex had told her of Josh's power, and how he was just beginning to understand it himself. She knew how quickly Josh could lose control of the risen dead, and hoped he was strong enough to keep them in the ground.

From behind, the growling of the wolves followed by the sheriff's aborted scream urged them on faster. When the main road appeared through the steady downpour, Glory felt relief flush through her body. She had never expected to return to Belkin's Pass, and she never imagined she would be glad to see it once again. The town had given her nothing but pain, and yet, here she was riding hard for its cluster of buildings to save her life.

Nightshade's hooves slipped a few times in the mud of the road, and flecks of foam from his mouth drifted back on the wind to spatter her legs. Glory risked a look back over her shoulder, blinking through the rain. The road led off into darkness, and she took a cautiously relieved breath. Then a flash of lightning revealed two figures following at a fast pace with wolves at their sides. Glory faced forward again, heart racing, and shouted to Josh just ahead of her, "They're behind us!"

Beneath a blinding flash of lightning and deep rumble of thunder, they arrived in the center of town and dismounted. Glory's feet sank up to her ankles in mud, and she followed Josh's lead, slapping her horse's rump and sending him off into the night. She noticed Josh spare his horse a concerned glance, and reached out to grab his upper arm.

"Where to?" Glory asked.

"Inside somewhere," he replied. "But we have to be sure they can't enter."

"Glory!"

The voice, high and trembling, barely cut through the wind-slanted rain. Glory spun in place, looking at the dark storefronts in turn along the raised boardwalk, searching for the caller. A lantern flickered in the dark, catching her eye. She pointed, but then stopped as she recognized the building.

Sally, the hard as flint owner of the One-Eyed Rooter, stood in the doorway of her saloon, waving them inside. She had charged Glory an outrageous rent for her tiny room upstairs, and then doubled or tripled it when she felt Glory had misbehaved. The woman was thin as a stick, subsisting on absinthe and very little else, but she packed power behind her slaps, a fact Glory could attest to first hand.

And she was not to be trusted.

"There!" Josh ran toward the lantern and Glory let out a curse.

"Josh! No!" But he didn't hear her over the wind and the rain. With another curse, Glory followed after him, her movements slow as her feet sank in the mud.

She caught up to him at the bottom of the steps leading to the boardwalk that fronted the saloon, and he turned to look at her, rain streaming off his hat. Glory shook her head and said, "We can't trust her."

Sally stepped out on the boardwalk beneath the over-hang. The flame inside her lantern flickered and died in a gust of wind, but a flash of lightning outlined her bony frame beneath the long silk dress the wind pressed against her.

She reached a trembling hand out to them. "Glory, come inside. You'll be safe from him, I promise."

Glory fixed the woman with a hateful look. "You're a liar, Sally. Balthazar's stench is all over the saloon. He turned Anne, Edith, Carmen, and Laura."

"Not my rooms," Sally said. "He's not been in my private rooms. We'll be safe there." She turned to look back along the street and her eyes widened. "They're coming! Hurry!"

Glory and Josh looked down the street at the dark, drenched figures rushing from building to building. Wolves followed on the heels of each figure, snarling and digging at doors and windows.

"We have to decide," Josh said.

"I'll see you dead if you're lying to us," Glory shouted, pointing a finger in Sally's face. "I swear it."

With a breath, Glory pulled her feet up from the sucking mud and climbed the steps to follow Sally into the One-Eyed Rooster.

FOUR

Glory and Josh followed Sally through the overturned tables and broken chairs of the One-Eyed Rooster. Lightning distorted their shadows along the walls. At the narrow staircase, Sally hiked her skirt an inch and climbed to the second level. As Glory followed, she could not help looking along the second floor balcony to the door of her old room where she had once slept and entertained men. The doors were all shut, and she looked at each in turn, her gaze lingering on the door to Edith's room.

Edith had been her only real friend over the years. Glory thought about the night she had found Balthazar bent over Edith's still, pale body. His mouth had been clamped hard on her neck, and the runners of blood trickling over her shoulder looked black in the moonlight. Balthazar had turned the other saloon girls into blood drinking demons like him, and they had attacked Glory the night she had escaped.

Glory reached the top of the steps and stood for a moment, hands fisted at her sides, her teeth clenched as she thought about the girls who had lived in those rooms. She had listened to them laugh and flirt with the men downstairs, and then heard them moan encouragement to those same men up in their rooms. She had heard them talk over breakfast about their dreams of marriage and children and a life outside the saloon, their faces drawn and lined in the hard light of morning. And now they were drinkers of blood who would perish in sunlight.

A door halfway down the second floor balcony creaked open an inch. Glory took two steps back, bumping into Josh as he came up the steps behind her.

"What is it?" Josh asked.

Glory pointed. "Someone's in that room."

"Come on!" Sally whispered, waving them toward her private rooms that lay to the right of the stairs, away from the doors to the girls' rooms. "Hurry."

Glory turned toward Sally's room, her gaze caught by the sparkle of a cut glass doorknob in a flash of lightning. She pushed Josh toward Sally and followed quickly behind him, her wet petticoats sticking to her legs as she walked.

A creak of hinges behind her brought her to a stop. Before she could turn around, Glory heard heavy footsteps pounding along the balcony floor toward her. Ohanzee's warmth burst around her, and she relaxed her muscles as she had learned to do under his protection all these years. He eased her back out of the way as a large figure stumbled past, a heavy, pale arm just missing her shoulders.

Josh stopped outside Sally's door and spun around. He held up the small cross that hung on a chain around his neck, a gift from Dex that had saved his life once already.

"Stay where you are!" Josh shouted.

Sally had again lit her lantern and now held it up beside Josh, throwing a wide yellow glow over the hallway. Glory looked down at the figure on its hands and knees between herself and Josh, relieved at the sight of the overburdened corset and long, frizzy hair.

"Beatrice?" she said in a gentle voice.

The girl turned to look at Glory over her shoulder. Tears sparkled in the lamp light, leaving tracks on Beatrice's dirty face. "Glory? It's really you? You come back to save us?"

"Is she safe?" Josh asked, looking between Glory and Sally.

"Well, I don't really know," Sally muttered. "She spends all of her time locked in her room."

Beatrice pushed to her feet and faced Glory. She held a chair leg with a sharpened end in one hand and a fifth of whiskey in the other. The dirt-stained corset struggled to contain her large breasts, and her bare shoulders were covered with scratches and bruises. Two inflamed red dots marked her neck.

"You're bit," Glory whispered, safe within Ohanzee's protection.

"Once," Beatrice said and a muscle in her jaw twitched as a stubborn look came into her eyes. "It won't happen again."

"She's bit?" Josh asked.

Glory met his gaze. "Just once. She won't turn." Josh returned her stare a moment then nodded, and Glory held out her hand to Beatrice. "Come on."

Beatrice let out a breath and tucked the chair leg under an arm so she could take Glory's hand. The girl's fingers were cool, and Glory gave her hand a reassuring squeeze before hurrying after Josh into Sally's rooms.

Dark green velvet covered the furniture and hung in heavy drapes at the windows and around the four-poster bed. Glory had only been inside the rooms once, the day Sally had hired her on at the One-Eyed Rooster four months before, and nothing had changed. A smell of anise lay heavy in the room, testament to Sally's fondness for absinthe.

"Are we truly safe in here?" Josh demanded of Sally, following her across the room to where she placed the lantern on a small tea table by the window.

She turned to him, her sunken and drawn face looking like a skull in the shadows thrown by the lantern. "I told you it was safe. If you don't believe me, you're free to return to the street." Lightning flashed outside the window, punctuating her remark, and Josh stepped away from her.

With a satisfied nod, Sally turned to Glory and Beatrice. "Take off your wet clothes. I've got some dry things here for you to wear."

"Glory?" Beatrice asked in a quiet, nervous voice.

Glory felt Ohanzee's warmth fade from around her now that the danger had passed, and she pulled her wet hair back as she looked into the girl's wide, freckled face. "Yes, Beatrice?"

"Am I going to become like the other girls?" Beatrice sat heavily on a small ottoman, the chair leg she carried clattering to the floor between her big feet. "A demon that drinks blood? Is that going to be what I become?"

Glory shook her head and squeezed Beatrice's shoulder. "No. You only got bit once, right?"

Beatrice nodded. "Just the one time." Her face clouded with anger, and she clenched her fists. "They caught me by the outhouse. Sneaky fuckers."

"From what I've been told, it takes three bites to turn you." Glory stepped behind the changing screen and peeled off her wet dress. "We'll keep you safe, Beatrice."

Sally appeared around the corner of the changing screen, a dress and a towel hanging over her arm, and a stern look on her face. "Don't make promises you can't keep, Glory."

Glory grabbed the towel and turned away to dry herself, pressing the dampness from her long hair. She lowered her voice to a whisper and said, "She needs hope, Sally. Everyone else in town is either hiding, dead, or been turned into a vampire." She draped the towel over the top of the screen and took the dress from Sally, holding it up against her. It was out of style but a good fit and weight against the September chill. Best of all, it was dry. She turned away from Sally's gaze to step into the dress and pull it up to her shoulders, only then realizing it buttoned up the back.

Sally came up behind her and pulled the material together, skillfully fastening the buttons up the back as if locking Glory inside the dress. "They're cunning liars, Glory. Those vampires. Cunning. They promise things in the night. Things you want, things you need." She continued to button up the dress, the collar tightening around Glory's throat. "The town is in disarray. As a woman on her own, I need to make sure I am taken care of, that I can survive. You, of all the girls, should respect my predicament, being a half-breed as you are. There. All buttoned up."

Glory faced Sally and searched the woman's eyes. She saw the desperation burning within them, and her stomach clenched and rolled with anxiety. Taking a quick breath, she clutched her hands together to keep from strangling the woman. "What have you done?"

Sally walked quickly away from her, saying over her shoulder, "I don't know what you mean."

Glory strode up behind her and grabbed Sally by the shoulder, spinning her around. The slap came as no surprise;

Sally had managed to slap her several times in the past. Glory had learned over the months she had worked for the woman that Ohanzee had trouble reading Sally. Glory attributed it to Sally's prolonged use of absinthe. Usually, Sally's slaps merely stung, but tonight Sally wore a ring that cut into Glory's cheek and left a fresh scrape.

"I have offered you shelter," Sally said, eyes burning with self-righteousness. She looked over at Josh who stood by the window, watching their interaction with intense interest. "I have brought you in from the cold and the rain." She looked at Beatrice slouched on the ottoman. "I have kept you safe from the murderous hordes outside these walls." She looked back at Glory, her eyes still alight. "I have given you the clothes off my back, and this is how you thank me? With accusations and insinuations?"

Anger surged through Glory, warming her, sharpening her senses, and she took a step closer. "I'll ask you one more time, Sally. What have you done?"

"What's going on?" Josh asked from the window.

"She cain't be trusted," Beatrice moaned. She took a pull from the whiskey bottle and put her head in her hands. "She cain't. She consorts with them. I hear them in the night, whispering."

"Shut your fool mouth, Beatrice," Sally snapped. "You're a drunk, ignorant farm girl whose parents sold her out to be a whore."

"Hey," Josh said, taking a step toward them. "There's no call for that kind of talk."

Glory darted a quick look at Josh. "She's made a deal."

"A deal?"

"Yes, Josh, a deal." Glory moved even closer to Sally and this time the woman held her ground, her small eyes hard and justified as she stared back at her. "Didn't you, Sally? You made a deal for absinthe."

"You got no right to talk to me this way, Glory," Sally said, but her voice trembled at the end, as if just hearing the word "absinthe" ignited her craving. Glory knew she was right.

"We need to go," Glory said and looked at Josh. "Now."

She turned toward the door and came to a stop. The cut glass knob slowly turned, sparkling in the lamp light. An icy chill shook through her, a chill that even Ohanzee's warmth couldn't ease. Glory stepped back from the door as it swung open to reveal Balthazar standing just over the threshold. The light from the lantern lit sparks inside his glowing red eyes.

Beatrice cried out and moved to stand alongside Glory and Josh, holding the chair leg in one hand and the whiskey bottle in the other.

"Well, look what we have here," Balthazar said, his deep voice smooth and assured. "Some mice have stumbled into our trap, Sally."

Sally hurried to Balthazar's side, clinging to his arm and staring up into his face. "I got them inside. That's what you wanted, isn't it? It's like I promised."

Balthazar stepped into the room and closed the door behind him. He smiled at them as he patted Sally's hand where it trembled on his arm. "You did just as I wanted, Sally."

FIVE

Josh could not catch his breath.

Balthazar blocked the door, red eyes sliding from him to Glory to Beatrice and back.

"You gave us up!" Glory shouted at Sally, and as Josh looked at Glory from the corner of his eye, he could see the warm golden glow around her. An Indian brave turned in profile stood just behind her, shimmering within the glow as if he stood across a strong campfire from Josh. Every time Josh tried to look at him directly, however, the man vanished along with the yellow light.

"Why, look who's back," Balthazar said and, in a blur of movement, stood directly in front of Glory, staring into her eyes. "My favorite half-breed whore."

"Don't look at him Glory!" Josh shouted. "He'll bewitch you!"

"He can't do that to me," Glory said through clenched teeth. She stared defiantly into Balthazar's eyes, hands curled into fists at her sides. "And he knows it. Stay away from us." She looked from Balthazar to Sally. "That goes for the both of you."

"You'll never find peace, Glory," Sally said in a desperate tone. "Just stay and embrace what he's offering you. He wants to give you everlasting life. Think of it!"

Anger rolled through Josh's gut and pushed the words up his throat. "He's not offering life, you stupid bitch. He's taking it."

"But you could live forever," Sally said. "Stay young forever. Who doesn't want that?"

Beatrice had circled behind Balthazar and Sally and now rushed the vampire, the sharpened chair leg held high over her head. Josh thought the girl might be able to drive the stake through his back and into his heart, when Balthazar surprised them all by stepping aside, leaving Glory open to Beatrice's downward stroke.

"No!" Josh took a helpless step toward the two women, reaching out to them, trying to stop the inevitable. Just as Beatrice's hands came down, however, Glory moved as if she had been shoved aside, leaving Beatrice to stumble into a high backed armchair near the window. The makeshift stake stabbed into the cushion.

"My chair!" Sally cried.

Suddenly, Balthazar stood directly in front of Josh, red eyes trying to catch his gaze. Josh dropped his eyes and stepped back from the chill that rolled off the man.

"You are strong willed," Balthazar whispered. "And your blood thrums with power." He leaned close, the cold of his presence like the touch of river ice, his lips an inch above Josh's neck. He paused to draw in a deep breath. "You smell familiar. Very familiar. I must have drained one of your relatives. I wonder if you'll taste the way you smell."

Josh lifted the cross that hung out of sight inside his shirt and pressed it to Balthazar's left cheek. The vampire cried out and leaped back, his cheek smoking and sizzling. In the glow of the lantern, Josh saw the flesh where the cross had touched him was black. Balthazar gently touched his cheek and lifted a corner of his lip in a snarl as he glared at Josh, his eyes red as flames. "You will pay for that."

The door behind Balthazar slammed open and a man stood in the frame, eyes glowing red, his chin and the front of his white shirt soaked with blood. It took Josh a moment before he recognized Pastor Blanton. The pastor stepped into the room, crouched beside Balthazar and hissed at them.

The sound of breaking glass drew everyone's attention toward the window as Beatrice used the sharpened chair leg to clear the frame of jagged pieces before stepping out onto the gently sloped roof. Rain swept in, soaking Sally's finely upholstered chairs and velvet drapes. Sally screamed as though in physical pain.

"You careless pig of a girl!" she shouted. "Look what you're doing to my things!" She ran across the room and reached out into the rain to grab Beatrice's arm.

"Fuck you and your things," Beatrice said, struggling to get loose from Sally. As the two wrestled within the window frame, Sally's arm dragged across a stray piece of glass. Releasing Beatrice, she cried out and stumbled backward, blood seeping through her fingers as she clutched the wound.

"No!" Balthazar snapped, grabbing Josh's attention. Josh instinctively held up his cross for protection, but it was Sally who was in danger.

The pastor smelled the fresh blood and leaped on Sally, knocking her face down on the floor. He twisted her arm up and back at an awkward angle. Sally cried out and struggled to get free, but Pastor Blanton was strong and hungry. He put one foot on her back, holding her down as he clamped his mouth over the open wound.

"Come on!" Beatrice shouted. Josh pushed Glory toward the window, backing away from Sally and her attacker as Balthazar stomped across the room to knock Pastor Blanton aside.

"Leave her!" Balthazar roared. "Her blood is poison."

"No!" Sally cried out, reaching toward Josh with her uninjured arm. "Take me with you! Please!"

Josh shook his head at her as he climbed backward out the window, his one bootless foot slipping on the rain-slick tiles as he struggled to hold up the cross. "You've made your deal."

"I could kill you in seconds," Balthazar sneered, his fingers straying to the mark of the cross now branded into his cheek. "But I'll let you have this moment of victory. I still have someone important to you. You will come to me soon enough."

Anger rose in Josh, blinding him, pushing him back through the window toward Balthazar. "You leave Dex be!"

"Josh, no!" Glory grabbed his arm and pulled him back outside. "Not now. Come on. We need to go."

Josh looked around and saw Beatrice already making her way along the roof toward the front of the saloon. Glory tugged him along. "Come on, Josh. It's not time yet. We'll get Dex soon, but not tonight. Not here."

Balthazar stood to the side of the window, red eyes tracking Josh until he was out of sight. Sally's moans and pleas for rescue grew muffled and were finally drowned out altogether by the rain and wind. Josh came to the edge of the roof and looked down. Glory and Beatrice stood on the roof of the boardwalk overhang several feet lower. Josh glanced back toward the window, saw no sign of pursuit, and jumped down to stand shivering beside them.

"Where to?" he asked with another glance back to watch for Balthazar. So far the vampire was letting them get away, which made Josh uneasy.

"Down." Glory stepped to the edge and dropped to the mud below, bending her knees and rolling out of the fall.

"No other choice!" Beatrice said to him and stepped off the roof as well.

Josh followed, the impact rattling through his body and making his teeth click together. He rolled onto his side, cold mud smearing along his side and back, his one bootless foot chilled to the point it was nearly numb. He stood up and looked around to get his bearings, startled to find Glory and Beatrice already running down the street. He followed the women, struggling to pull his feet from the mud as he tried to look everywhere at once, alert for wolves and vampires. The vacant street both relieved and concerned him. Where had the group that attacked the sheriff and deputy gone?

He caught up with Glory and Beatrice at a corner, huddled out of the rain against the wall of the bank beneath the overhang.

"Where can we go?" Glory asked. Her arms were crossed, and she shivered in the biting wind.

"We gotta get outta the rain." Beatrice's voice shook as her teeth chattered. She wore only the corset, the chemise beneath, and her petticoats. Her bare, pale shoulders trembled in the night wind.

"We need to find a place the vampires would never be able to enter," Josh said. "Someplace they've never been invited."

"How we gonna know that?" Beatrice asked. "I been afraid to leave my room since Glory run off. I don't know where they been inside and where they ain't."

Glory looked up and down the street, and, in a flash of lightning, Josh saw her gaze lock on something. A smile curled up one corner of her mouth. It softened her face, making her look beautiful even beneath the mud and rain.

"I know where we can go," Glory said. "Follow me."

CHAPTER

SIX

When the screaming finally stopped, Dex had stretched out on the hard stone floor. He had no idea if it was day or night, but he was exhausted. The cut along his forearm seeped blood but had, for the most part, scabbed over. Each time he moved his arm the skin pulled, however, and made him hiss with pain. Balthazar had squeezed that arm so tight it felt as if his cold fingers still gripped it.

Dex closed his eyes and gathered thoughts of Josh in his mind. He remembered the few times they had been naked together, sucking each other, Dex fucking him. It had felt so right, so natural. Dex knew they were meant to be together, and he wished he had told Josh about his feelings sooner. But things in the past were best left there, as his father used to say.

He drifted off to sleep and dreamed of Josh. They were back in the cabin where Josh had been born, where he had lived with his mother, Maureen, before she vanished. It stood empty and dark, the wide expanse of Venom Valley stretching away outside the windows, and Dex lay nude on his back across the old iron-framed bed.

Wet, slick heat engulfed Dex's cock, and he grunted as Josh lowered his mouth over him. He paused a moment, Dex's entire length deep in his throat, then Josh moved his mouth slowly up and down. Dex had his arms stretched overhead to clutch the iron headboard as he writhed beneath Josh. He felt Josh's hands moving up his torso, fingers parting the hair on his chest as the speed of his mouth increased.

A flicker of heat started deep inside his groin, and his muscles clenched. Dex tightened his grip on the rungs of the headboard and turned his head back and forth as his climax built and Josh continued to suck him.

Suddenly, the heat of Josh's mouth was gone, the chill air in the room cooling his glistening cock. Dex raised his head and looked down to see Josh standing beside the bed, his gaze locked on Dex as he unbuttoned and stripped off his shirt. In a moment, Josh was naked, his cock standing tall and thick from its patch of dark blond hair. The light from the nearby candle glinted in the drop of slick that dripped from the tip and Dex licked his lips, eager for a taste.

But Josh had other ideas. He turned away to swipe his fingers in a small bowl and rubbed something slick and warm on Dex's cock.

"What is it?" Dex asked.

"Lard." Josh smiled and winked. "Grease you up like a roasted pig, Dexter Wells."

"Grease away," Dex said and closed his eyes. He adjusted his grip on the headboard, and his cock jerked with excitement when the mattress dipped and Josh straddled him.

"Ready?" Josh asked.

"I've been ready for years," Dex replied. He tried to keep the raw emotion out of his voice, but knew he hadn't done a good job of it.

A brief resistance met the hooded tip of Dex's cock and then, with a sudden push, he was past the tight ring of Josh's opening. The heat of Josh's body closed around him like a long, tight fist as Dex seated himself inside Josh. He opened his eyes and looked up into Josh's face, took in the dark blond hair damp with sweat, the soft shadows thrown by the candle flame, the curve of his jaw, and the line of his teeth barely visible between parted lips. Dex ached to touch Josh, feel his skin beneath his fingers, rub his thumbs across Josh's nipples and take the hard shaft slapping against his belly in hand.

But for some reason, Dex couldn't let go of the headboard.

Josh seemed to understand this even though Dex did not, and he moved atop Dex. Grounding his ass down, he took Dex deep inside, then rose up and dropped down again. Dex lifted his hips to meet Josh on the down stroke, driving his cock into Josh's body, spearing him to what felt like his absolute center, as though Dex had touched a spot inside Josh that no other man ever could.

The force of his thrust pushed a grunt from Josh's lips and he fell forward over Dex to run his hands along Dex's tightened arms and down his chest. Josh kissed him, his lips cold from the chilly air around them, tongue pushing between his lips and filling Dex's mouth. All the while, Josh continued to move on top of Dex, took him deep and lifted up to sit down on him again.

Dex's climax came suddenly, and he grunted a warning into Josh's eager mouth as they kissed. Josh moved his hips faster, slamming down onto him until Dex exploded inside

Josh with a strangled cry. His hips lifted, thrusting deep as he pumped his seed inside Josh's willing body.

Josh held Dex inside him, one hand braced on Dex's chest, the other stroking himself. As his climax neared, Josh's fingers tightened and released against Dex's skin, gently tugging the fine hairs on his chest.

"I'm close," Josh whispered, his voice heavy and hoarse. "God, I love having you inside me."

"Come on," Dex said through clenched teeth. He lifted his hips high, pushing deep into Josh, his cock still hard even after his release.

A moment later, Dex heard Josh's gasp and the hot, thick flood of his release splashed across his chest. The familiar sharp odor filled the air, and Dex wished he could lower his hands to run his fingers through it, lift it to his lips, and swallow it down.

But his hands seemed stuck over his head. His fingers gripped the headboard tight, unable to release their hold no matter how hard he tried. Dex focused all his strength on pulling his hands free, but it was no use. Exhausted, he let out a frustrated huff and looked down to find Balthazar sitting on top of him in place of Josh.

Dex jumped and tried to throw the vampire off, but Balthazar was too strong. He held on tight with his thighs as his cold internal muscles gripped Dex's cock like an icy fist.

"No!" Dex shouted up at Balthazar. "This is a trick! I would never do this with you!"

Balthazar smiled down at him, pointed teeth gleaming in the yellow candlelight. "Oh, but you will, Dexter Wells. You will."

The vampire's mouth opened wide, then wider still, until it gaped above him, impossibly huge. Dex shouted for Josh, for help, for anyone, but there was no one. He was alone, and his scream went unnoticed as Balthazar lowered his mouth to Dex's neck.

And bit.

Dex awoke with a strangled shout, kicking his feet and pulling at the chains that secured him to the stone wall. A dream, that's all it had been. Just a dream. He lay alone, chained in the dark in Balthazar's cave.

Dex had shifted during his dream, and his arms were now tangled in the heavy chains above his head. In his thrashings, the metal cuff on his left wrist had slipped up to the last joint of his thumb. It was painful, but... it had slipped. Dex twisted his hand within the cuff. Was there enough play between the cuff and his hand? Could he, if he pulled hard enough, get that hand free?

He paused to listen for any sound of movement, but all that came to him was the woman in another cavern nearby. She had stopped screaming, thankfully, and now babbled quietly to herself, the words unintelligible as they echoed around the cave walls. Dex had lost track of time since he had been chained inside the cave, and he didn't know how long he had been held, or if it was day or night outside. If it were night, Balthazar would be out hunting, but returning soon. If the sun was up, he would be sleeping, but awakening soon.

Either way, Dex didn't want to stay here another moment longer. He took a few deep breaths and pulled against the cuff with all his strength. The metal edge dug into his thumb, making him grit his teeth as it peeled up a few layers of skin and greased the metal with blood.

He paused and caught his breath then pulled again, harder this time. Just as he thought it wouldn't work, the thumb on his left hand popped out of its socket, and his hand pulled free of the cuff. Dex cried out once, then stifled his pain as he held his left hand to his chest. The screaming woman had fallen silent while he had struggled to escape, but she cried out to echo his pain, mocking him.

"Quiet!" Dex shouted, then more quietly, "Please! Be quiet. For just a while." He gently touched his hand in the dark. The thumb needed to be put back in place, but doing that in the dark of the cave wasn't a good idea.

Dex followed the chain to the wall and pulled it through the ring secured to the stone. The left cuff rattled toward him across the cave floor and up the wall to strike the ring. Dex cursed and pulled on the chain with his right hand, trying to force it through, but the cuff was too large to fit through the ring.

Though not completely free, Dex now had a lot more chain to move about his small cavern. Keeping his left hand tucked close to his chest, Dex felt his way along the wall to the small outcropping of rock where he touched the candle Balthazar had lit on his first visit. He found a box of matches near the base and, in a moment, Dex had lit the wick and leaned down beside it to examine his thumb.

It laid across his palm, bruised and swollen, blood drying along the spots where the skin had peeled away. Dex grabbed the thumb in his right hand, took several deep breaths, and jerked it back into place. The pain made him cry out and sent him to his knees, leaving him dizzy and his stomach rolling. If he'd had any food recently, he would have thrown it up. The woman screamed along with him, and then giggled madly, but he ignored her as he fought to get his breath back.

His right hand still locked in the metal cuff, he pushed

himself to his feet, grabbed the candle off the rock and inched forward. The chain allowed him to go as far as the entrance to a narrow passage, down which he could see the muted glow of another candle. He figured the screaming woman was down there.

A tug on the chain granted him another few inches. He stepped out into the passage and held the candle out in front of him, watching the flame. It didn't move when he held it in the direction of the screaming woman, but when he held it out the other way, the flame flickered in a tiny breath of a draft.

Freedom lay in that direction.

With renewed determination, Dex grabbed a palm-sized stone from the passage and crossed his tiny cavern back to the wall. He pulled the chain through until the left cuff lay on the stone floor, then he held it in place with his foot on the chain. Raising the stone in his right hand, he brought it down on the metal cuff with as much strength as he could muster. The impact with the cuff rattled through the stone and along his arm, sending sparks of pain shooting out from his injured forearm. But Dex had little time and could not hesitate. He had no idea how long he had until Balthazar returned or awoke.

He lost count of how many times he struck the cuff, but soon it lay dented and misshapen at his feet. Dex quickly pulled the chain through the ring, holding his breath as he watched the cuff bump along the floor and up the stone wall. It caught on the ring at first, but with some maneuvering, Dex was able to force it through.

He was free. He still had one hand attached to a long length of chain, but he was free.

Dex looped as much of the chain as he could around his

right hand. He winced as he forced his left thumb to grip the candle then moved into the dark passage outside his cavern. The last few feet of chain dragged the mangled cuff along the stone behind him.

The candle flickered with his movements, throwing shadows that made him jump as he crept along the passage toward the soft glow of light where the screaming woman waited. A few times the dragging cuff caught between rocks and jerked him to a stop, forcing him to retrace his steps and free it.

All the while the woman ahead of him continued to scream.

Dex came to a corner and pressed himself against the wall. The glow of a candle and the sound of the woman's screams assured him he was just feet away. Weighed down by the loops of chain, he had no idea what he would do once he finally stood before her, but he had to try and help.

He had devised a vague plan of finding somewhere to hide inside the cave until Balthazar awoke and left to hunt or daylight drove him back to sleep. But before he found a place to hide, he had to see the screaming woman. Maybe he could help her. Or maybe she could help him. He wouldn't be able to survive long in Venom Valley carrying a heavy chain.

Rounding the corner, Dex stepped into a wide, open space. He held up the candle and the light picked out furniture, including a tall bed with a mattress, ornate vases and place settings, and paintings lined up to lean against the walls. Off in a corner rested a long wooden coffin, lovingly polished and elaborately decorated with what appeared to be gold inlay. That must have been where Balthazar slept during the day. Dex shuddered and turned to find another cavern, this one a little larger than his own. Several candles burned from different places on the rocks, piles of melted wax hoisting the tapers high into the air.

And then he stood staring at the woman who had, until he stepped into view, been screaming almost nonstop.

She sat in a comfortable armchair, her wrists cuffed just as Dex's had been, mouth open and eyes wide. Pale skin covered jutting bones, a testament to the length of time she had been Balthazar's captive, and Dex fleetingly wondered why she was being held instead of killed or turned to join his growing army. Before he could fully follow that train of thought, however, Dex's gaze was caught by the woman's hair.

It was white as mountain snow and fell straight down her back to lie in a pile on the floor. Dex ran his gaze up the flow of hair until he came back to the woman's face, and his heart stuttered in his chest. The shape of her face, the way her chin narrowed to a softly rounded point, and the light brown color of her eyes left Dex momentarily out of breath. Could it be?

"Maureen?" Dex whispered.

The woman screamed at him, her voice shrill and agonizing now that he stood this close to her. Her brown eyes looked through him, as if she didn't really see him there at all. He would never be able to get her out of the cave. And even if he did, Balthazar had held her here for so long, her mind was gone.

Dex turned to go back the way he had come, but stopped at the sight of Balthazar standing at the bend in the passage. The light of Dex's candle illuminated the mark of a cross burned into his cheek. The vampire's red eyes gleamed in the yellow glow, and one fang was visible within his half smile.

"I see you managed to get loose," Balthazar said, his voice deep and smooth, his accent soothing Dex's tense nerves.

Before Dex could move, Balthazar stood directly before him, red eyes boring into his, filling Dex's vision, digging into his brain, his heart, his soul.

"You would not have made it very far with this heavy chain to carry." Balthazar slipped the chain off Dex's arm and let it fall to the stone floor. "So determined to leave. And yet, nowhere for you to go. Your friends were taken by your peacekeeper back to that patch of ground you called home."

"Sheriff Haden," Dex heard himself say. He tried to look away from Balthazar's eyes, tried to come back inside himself, but he couldn't move, couldn't think. He lived only to answer Balthazar's demands.

Balthazar took a step closer and gripped Dex by the shoulders, his red eyes filling Dex's vision and becoming his world.

"You know who gave me this nasty burn, Dexter Wells?"

"No."

"Your special friend did this."

"Josh."

"Yes, Josh." Balthazar leaned closer, as if to share a secret and Dex listened hard because he needed to know everything Balthazar wanted to tell him. "I want you to tell me what you know about Josh."

Dex saw the glow of Balthazar's eyes, red as an autumn sunset. He thought about Josh, conjured up the sight of his face, felt the now familiar lines of his body beneath his hands. Josh was safe, he could sense that. Safe and out of Balthazar's reach. The certainty of this feeling steeled Dex's will, helped him push back against Balthazar's control.

"Josh is a good man," Dex said. "He's safe."

Balthazar leaned in even closer. "But you know things about Josh, Dexter Wells. Tell me those things; tell me Josh's secrets. It is all right. He will never find out it was you who told me."

Dex shook his head. "No. Josh is safe and good."

Balthazar moved back, rising to his full height above Dex. "I see. Well, Deputy, I was hoping it would not come to this, but you leave me no choice. I have returned from this brutal attack by your friend Josh to find you wandering loose in my home. And here you stand in front of my experiment of many years as if you mean to take her away with you. That kind of thing cannot go unpunished, now can it?"

Fear spiked into Dex's belly. "I got free. But I won't do it again."

Balthazar smiled, his pointed teeth wickedly sharp in the glow of the candle. "Oh, I know you won't. Just know that this is going to please me as much as it's going to hurt you." Balthazar's red eyes vanished from Dex's sight and a sharp, deep pain spiked into his neck.

Dex felt Balthazar's teeth in his neck, and he let out a scream that was matched by the white haired woman chained up behind him.

CHAPTER
SEVEN

Glory woke to the morning sun. She sat up instantly alert, her heart beating fast. It took a moment for her to remember where she was, then the events of the previous night came back to her as well. As she looked around, she relaxed somewhat. Her back was stiff from sleeping on the hard wooden bench, and a muscle in her neck tightened in protest as she turned her head, but they had made it through the night.

Josh and Beatrice slept on benches not far away. Beyond them stood the church's pulpit and altar, and behind that a large stained glass window. It had been an expensive addition. She remembered hearing the men complaining of it in the Rooster what seemed like a lifetime ago, but Glory could see why the pastor had pushed for it. She had never been inside the church before—as part Apache and a saloon girl she had not been welcome, and had had no use for it—but now, awakening inside the building after the long night, with the morning sunlight setting the colored glass aflame, she felt calm. Safe.

For now.

She got up and walked to the doors at the back of the church where, as quietly as possible, she took apart the barricade they had set up the night before. Taking hold of a handle, Glory drew in a breath and pulled one of the doors open. A gentle breeze carried puffs of dust across the threshold to collide with the hem of her dress and fall on her shoes. She leaned out the door and peered up and down the street, then stepped out on the small porch. The air was crisp but warm for mid-September, the road still muddy from the storm the night before.

Ohanzee's spirit was quiet for now, letting her know danger was not close at hand. The street was unusually empty, and in the morning light, Glory could see the full extent of the damage the town had suffered. A number of stores up and down the street had shattered windows, and the general store's doors had been broken in. Other than the damage, however, all seemed safe. Down at the opposite end of the street, Glory could see Sally's green velvet draperies hanging out of the window through which they had escaped Balthazar.

A horse snorted nearby and Glory leaned out over the porch steps to see Clementine and Nightshade standing at the water trough. Scratches and raw, red scrapes marred their flanks, but the horses had survived the night. Josh would be pleased to see his horse and, Glory had to admit, she was glad to see Nightshade.

"Anyone around?"

Glory jumped and turned, a hand to her chest to still her racing heart at the sight of Beatrice behind her.

"Just Josh and Dex's horses." Glory noticed that Beatrice

stood just out of the sunlight, blinking fiercely as she squinted against the light. "Does the sun hurt?"

"Not too bad." Beatrice said and turned watery, narrowed eyes to her. "It's from the bite, isn't it?"

"Most likely."

"Will it change me any more?"

"I don't know, Bea." Glory reached out to squeeze her arm. "But we'll help you as much as we can, all right?"

Glory turned away to step down to the road when Beatrice called out, "Glory?"

She looked up at her. "Yes?"

"You won't let me become one of them, will you?" Beatrice swallowed, and a tear spilled down her cheek. "You won't let me become a blood drinker, right?"

Glory met her gaze and shook her head. "I swear I won't let that happen."

Beatrice's shoulders lowered, and her face softened as she relaxed. "Thank you."

"I'm going to look around, okay?"

"Want me to come?"

Glory shook her head again. "No. Stay with Josh. I'll be all right."

And she would be all right, Glory knew. She had Ohanzee to protect her.

As she made her way down the center of the road, stepping around the deeper mud puddles and skirting two bodies, one human and the other a wolf, Glory thought back on the many times Ohanzee had protected her. Since her father had taken her into the woods not long after her sixth birthday, Ohanzee had been there to save her. At first, he appeared because of a variety of missteps on her part, keeping her safe from accidents. But as she grew older,

Glory started deliberately putting herself in danger just to see him, to feel the warmth of him, the fleeting physical touch of him. He became the one man Glory knew would never leave, not only because her father had bound his spirit to hers, but because she felt his love. It had grown strong over the years as she had matured, and she knew that if Ohanzee ever took physical form, he would still remain with her.

She pushed open the door to the clothing and dry goods store and called out a greeting. No one responded, so she stepped inside and walked the narrow aisles, fingers trailing over the dresses and men's clothing as she looked for a fresh set of clothes for each of them, and a pair of boots for Josh.

"Glory!"

She turned toward the window, watching Josh walk down the road, limping on his one bootless foot, the sock black with mud and blood. He narrowed his eyes as he scanned the buildings searching for her. She wondered where he found the shotgun he carried, but she was glad he had started to gather weapons. They would need to find many more before nightfall when the vampires and wolves returned.

Glory opened her mouth to call to him, but the empty store and the surrounding materials comforted her in a way that she had not felt for a long time. It was safe here, secure and quiet. Instead, she let Josh walk out of sight and turned her attention back to selecting several changes of clothes for all of them, lingering in the peace of the store.

A sound to her right made her jump, and she felt the sudden warm embrace of Ohanzee. He stood behind her, just over her left shoulder as usual, his presence soothing her racing heart. With him there to protect her, Glory's courage took her a few steps deeper into the store, closer to the shadowy hallway that led to the back room.

"Hello?" she called.

A man stepped out of the hallway, his face dirty and his eyes wide. He held a stack of men and women's clothing in his hands.

"Who are you?" the man asked.

"My name is Glory," she said as she took a cautious step back. "I don't mean any trouble. I'm just looking for clothes. Is this your store?"

"No ma'am," the man said. "I just needed things for me and my wife. She's not feeling well."

"I understand. I won't tell." Glory waved toward the empty street behind her. "I don't think anyone cares anymore."

The man nodded and turned away, headed for the back exit most likely. But then he paused and faced her again. "Have you heard 'em? The voices?"

"Voices?" Glory said. The way the man had turned back to her exposed a part of his neck that had been hidden by his collar, and Glory saw two red puncture marks in his pale skin.

"At night," the man said. "They whisper and promise sweet things." He blinked rapidly, as if coming out of a dream. "My wife thinks they're angels. But I don't think they are, do you?"

Glory felt Ohanzee press closer against her back. She knew the man couldn't see him there, but she could feel Ohanzee as a solid being, could make out the firm swell of his chest, the hard lines of his body.

"Glory!"

She jumped and looked toward the front of the store,

Ohanzee's hands a physical weight on her shoulders, ready to move her out of harm's way if needed. But it was only Josh standing in the shop doorway, the shotgun held across his chest and an angry expression on his face.

"You shouldn't have wandered off alone," Josh said. "It's not safe."

Glory searched the shadows at the back of the store, but the man was gone.

"You all right?" Josh asked.

"Yes," Glory said. She felt a chill in the air as Ohanzee's presence faded, and he left her alone once again.

Josh sighed and looked down at the boardwalk a moment. "Sorry I raised my voice at you. I just think it would be best for us to tell each other where we're going."

Glory nodded and reached out to gather shirts and pants. "I picked out some clothes for us." She lifted her chin in the direction of the boots. "Boots are there."

Josh looked around the store with a guilty expression and Glory shook her head before saying, "There's no one left to pay, Josh. It's not stealing, it's need."

He nodded and stepped up to the boots. After holding a couple of boots to the bottom of his foot for measurement, he picked out a pair and headed for the door. Holding the clothes against her chest, Glory stepped out onto the board-walk and then down into the muddy road where Josh fell into step beside her.

"The horses are back," Josh said.

Glory nodded as she stepped around a puddle. "I saw them. We should get the saddles off."

"I did that already. Led them to the feed store and got them to eat, too." They walked on in silence a bit, and then

Josh said, "It was a good idea you had last night. Staying in the church, I mean. Vampires don't like holy ground."

"Let's hope the wolves don't either," she said.

"We'll need to reinforce the windows today after we look for other survivors."

She thought about the young man she had just met in the store. In another night or two, he would be a vampire coming out at night to hunt them down. "We should check the outer farms as well. If there are no survivors, we might find vampires in root cellars or under houses out of the sun."

Josh nodded. "True."

Back at the church, they all changed into the clean, dry clothes. Glory had grabbed a wide range of sizes of breeches and shirts for her and Beatrice. No more restrictive corsets or long dresses that would tangle around their legs. They all needed to be able to move and fight. Once changed, they made their way through town to check the other buildings for supplies. Beatrice stopped in the milliner's shop for a hat to keep the sun off her face, but soon stomped back outside with her head still bare.

"What's wrong?" Glory asked.

"They're all too fancy for my taste," Beatrice said and waved her arm back toward the store. "Feathers and lace and veils and whatnot. I just need a plain hat to keep the sun off my face. Is that too much to ask?"

Glory managed to keep from laughing and took Beatrice by the arm. "Let's try another store."

GLORY GUIDED Beatrice toward the blacksmith shop, and they pulled aside one of the double doors built wide enough to admit a horse and wagon. The forge was dark, and the smell of horse and metal hung heavy in the still, shadowed air.

"What are we doing in here?" Beatrice whispered. "I ain't wearing no metal hat."

"Smithy Donegan also does leather work," Glory explained as she made her way to the back of the work area. "See here? There are some plains hats with wide brims, perfect to keep the sun out of your eyes."

"Don't fuckin' move."

The voice came from directly behind them, and the command was followed by the sound of a gun being cocked. Glory looked over her shoulder as Ohanzee's spirit surrounded her. Edgar Donegan, known throughout town as Smithy Donegan, or simply Donegan, stood in the shadows holding two revolvers, one trained on each of them.

"Donegan, it's me, Glory," she said, and slowly turned to face him. "From the One-Eyed Rooster."

He was a tall man, heavy with muscle from years of hammering iron. His face was coated with soot and sweat, making the blue of his eyes stand out even more as he squinted at her. "Glory? That you?"

Glory nodded, relieved that he remembered her. It had been a long time since Donegan had set foot in the Rooster. Some said he was sweet on a girl in town, others said he got religion and stopped drinking and whoring. Whatever the reason, Glory had been surprised to find that she had missed the man. He never caused trouble, and he treated every girl with respect.

"You breakin' into my smithy?" Donegan asked, the guns still pointed at them.

"Ain't you been lookin' outside?" Beatrice said, her voice

loud in the shadowy, quiet expanse of the building. "It's war out there."

"War? With who? Injuns?"

Glory let that comment go. Now was not the time to debate which people were the more war-hungry.

Josh stepped up behind the blacksmith and pressed the end of the double-barreled shotgun against the back of Donegan's skull. He drew back both hammers and said in a calm voice, "Turn the guns around and hand one to each of the women. Now."

Glory saw Donegan swallow hard before he eased the hammers of both guns back into place and turned them around. She and Beatrice each took a gun and Donegan raised his hands over his head.

"Take what you want and go," Donegan said, his voice shaking. "I ain't got much, but just take it."

Josh stepped back from him and reseated the hammers of his shotgun. "Turn around."

Donegan did as he was told, and his eyes widened at the sight of him. "Josh Stanton? You got some balls to come back into town, what with a bounty on your head for murder."

"Well, I didn't do it." Josh lowered the shotgun. "Put down your hands and tell us what's been going on here in town."

In a tired voice, Donegan told them about the disappearances and the screams he'd been hearing in the night. The wolves and vandals the night before had been the first time he'd seen any sign of wrongdoing.

"They'll be back," Josh said. "And they're not vandals, they're vampires."

Donegan squinted at him in confusion. "Vampires? What's that?"

"They bewitch you and then they bite your neck and drink your blood," Beatrice said. She stepped up and pulled the collar of her shirt down to show off the scabbed wounds on her neck. Donegan sucked in a breath and took two steps back from her. Beatrice gave a short nod and continued. "You get bit three times and then you become like them." She looked over at Glory. "Ain't that right?"

Glory nodded. "Three bites and then you die. But you come back to life soon after, only different. You want to drink blood. Nothing else matters. You'll hurt anyone and everyone to satisfy it, even those you love."

"Demons," Donegan whispered. "How do you all know this?"

"The Apache tribe in the mountains around Venom Valley have been tracking the vampire Balthazar for a while now," Josh said. "They've seen what he can do, and they also know his weaknesses. Balthazar's been busy creating a lot of vampires like himself."

"He going to start a war?" Beatrice asked.

Josh shook his head. "I don't know, most likely. All I know for sure is he's taken Dex Wells."

"The deputy?" Donegan blurted.

Josh nodded. "Got him prisoner out in a cave somewhere in Venom Valley. I'm trying to figure out how to get out there and rescue him."

"Well, where's Sheriff Haden and Deputy Underwood?" Donegan asked.

"Dead," Glory replied, shaking her head when Donegan turned his terrified gaze her way. "We didn't kill them. It was the wolves and vampires. The vampires control the wolves."

"Dear God," Donegan whispered. "No one's safe."

"We are if we stick together," Josh said. "And the

vampires can't come out in the daylight, so we got time to prepare. Are you with us?"

Donegan looked between the three of them, and Glory made a point of lowering the revolver he had handed over. Finally, he looked back to Josh and nodded. "All right. I'll stand with you. Do you have enough guns?"

"The guns are only good against the wolves," Glory said. "Bullets don't hurt vampires."

"Bullets don't hurt 'em?" Donegan shook his head. "I ain't never heard of anything can stand up against a bullet. Say it's true though, how do you plan to fight 'em?"

"Silver," Josh said over his shoulder as he turned to the door. "You got any silver blades?"

Donegan let out a tired laugh. "You grew up in this town, Josh. You know there ain't much call for silver. No one can afford it."

"Maybe we could find some silver in some of the houses," Beatrice suggested. "Candlesticks or other fine things?" She noticed Donegan's look and said in a defensive tone, "They's most likely dead, Smithy Donegan, or a vampire anyway and unable to touch anything silver, so it ain't stealing."

"Not sure we could find enough silver to melt down," Josh said as he started to pace. "Most in the town have lived simple lives."

Glory watched him walk to the blacksmith's door to look up and down the street. Just as she was about to ask if he had any other ideas, Josh said over his shoulder, "Can you heat your forge enough to melt silver?"

Glory frowned and followed Donegan's gaze to the dark stone forge across the room.

"If you got enough coal," Donegan said. "I ain't got but a few buckets in the back. Mostly I use wood."

"There's coal at the train station," Beatrice said, and Glory turned to find her trying on hats. Beatrice noticed she suddenly had everyone's attention and gave an embarrassed shrug. "I used to wait there for one of the engineers sometimes. I seen big piles of coal out there for the trains."

"Okay, we got a coal supply," Glory said and turned back to Josh. "Now we just need the silver."

"Got that, too." Josh pointed out the door and down the street.

Glory followed Donegan to the door and heard Beatrice come up behind her. They all looked down the street and Donegan turned to gape at Josh.

"The bank?" Donegan let out a heavy gasp of surprise and walked off, hands in the air. "I ain't robbin' no bank, no matter how many Injuns or vampires or wolves there is. No sir."

Glory frowned at Josh. "You want to rob the bank? Are you serious?"

Josh turned his golden brown eyes on her and nodded once, his lips pressed into a thin, determined line. "I'm serious. We got to stop Balthazar somehow, and if a few bags of silver coins will help us do it before he takes over our town, and then the next town over, and the next one after that, then that's what we gotta do."

"Josh, we're already wanted by local law," Glory said. "Robbing a bank will put us on the federal list. Isn't there another way?"

"Do you know of one?" Josh asked, anger flashing in his eyes.

"You all fall off your horses and crack your skulls?"

Donegan asked. "That's bank robbin', and it ain't right. It ain't! We'd all go to jail for that, and I ain't goin' to jail to help you three out, no matter how many wolves and whatevers come out at night." He paced back and forth, chewing his lower lip as he swung his big hands before him. "It's stealin', that's what it is. And it ain't right. It's a sin to steal!"

Glory held her hands up toward Donegan in an attempt to get him to calm down. "Quiet down, Donegan. Quiet down." She looked at Josh. "There's got to be some other way."

Josh threw up his hands. "All right then, tell me. This is my idea, what's yours?"

Glory opened her mouth, found no words, and closed it. She looked to Beatrice and found her staring back, eyes wide and frightened. Glory risked a glance at Donegan and saw the man glaring at the floor of his smithy, strong arms folded over his broad chest and lips pressed tight as he shook his head.

"Well?" Josh demanded. "We're waiting."

Was there any other option? They had to stand too close to use wooden stakes, and they could only hide inside buildings for so long. Silver was the one thing they knew for sure that burned the vampires and cut their flesh.

Glory looked at the dirt floor beneath her muddy shoes. She let out her breath and with it, her resistance. She couldn't think of another way to battle the army Balthazar had gathered, as much as she hated it.

She took a breath, looked up to meet Josh's gaze, and nodded. "All right. What do we do?"

EIGHT

First, they had to convince Donegan about the vampires. They walked him through the streets, pointing out the damage caused by the wolves and vampires, and Josh even led him into a few empty buildings. The blacksmith wasn't convinced, and he kept trying to return to his shop to get back to work, calling them sinners and bank robbers.

Josh finally convinced Donegan to follow him to one more place and took him into one of the rooming houses. The building was empty, and Josh strode to the kitchen where he pulled up a rug to reveal the door to the root cellar. When he pulled up the door, the smell of damp and rotting vegetables wafted up to them, layered with something even more repulsive.

"Somethin' died down there," Donegan said, taking a step back. "Smells awful."

"Something dead is down there," Josh told him. "Most likely the residents of this rooming house."

Donegan's eyes widened. "Someone killed 'em and stuck 'em down there?"

"They're vampires," Josh said. "Like we've been telling you. They can't move during the daylight, so it's safe to come down with me."

Donegan's eyes widened even more. "You ain't goin' down there?"

Josh pulled the cross from within his shirt and held it up for Donegan to see. "I am with this. This burns 'em just as well as silver."

Donegan's face seemed to close up as he scowled at Josh. "Back to that bank robbin' again."

Taking a few steps down the cellar ladder, Josh looked up at the blacksmith. "Come down with me, let me show you. And bring that candle."

After Josh spent a few difficult minutes standing in the dark, rank root cellar alone, he was relieved to see Donegan's big boots clomp down the rungs of the ladder. The blacksmith had brought the candle, and he handed it over to Josh as his blue eyes darted from one shadowed corner to the other.

They found the bodies in the furthest corner from the ladder, stretched out on the dirt floor, awaiting sundown. Their skin was cold and pale, and their chests did not rise and fall with breath. Josh held his cross to the skin of a woman's hand where it sizzled and wisps of smoke drifted up. When he removed the cross, it left behind a black mark that made Donegan swallow hard.

"It burned her," Donegan whispered. "Like you said." He stared at the bodies laid out before them, then he looked at Josh. "What do we do now?"

"We have to drive a wooden stake into their hearts," Josh said.

"That's murder!" Donegan backed up toward the ladder.

"You have truly lost your mind, Josh Stanton. First you shot Agnes, we all know that. And you might have killed Sheriff Haden and Deputy Underwood for all's I know."

"Donegan!" Josh called his name in a sharp voice, and the man stopped his retreat to glare at him. "If I was to put a stake in a living person's heart, what would happen?"

"They'd die!"

"But they'd bleed, too, right?" Josh held the candle out to him. "They'd bleed red blood and die, yes? Watch closely."

He turned back to the bodies and drew a stake from the bag he carried over his shoulder. Holding it over the chest of a man whose name he had never learned while the man had been living, Josh took a breath before bringing it down hard. The man's eyes opened, burning red coals of pure hatred. He grabbed at Josh as thick black blood bubbled and poured from his mouth, his lips pulled back from pointed fangs.

Josh scooted back from the mess of blood and filth as the man's arms dropped, and his head fell back to the dirt. His skin flaked away, and his body crumbled in on itself as he turned to dust.

"Sweet Jesus," Donegan whispered.

"We have to kill as many of them as we can while the sun is up," Josh said. "Or they'll continue to create more vampires, and we'll lose not just Belkin's Pass, but every town out to each coast."

Donegan took a breath and fixed Josh with a hard gaze. "I don't got a quarrel with you, Josh Stanton. And I never talked about you or your Momma behind your back like them other folks in town. I was all for giving you a chance to make a new life with Agnes when she took you in."

Josh nodded and wiped sweat from his forehead,

wondering where Donegan was going with his speech. "I appreciate that, Donegan."

"But hear me clear right now." Donegan held up a thick, dirty finger. "If you are lying to me, I will turn you in to the law as fast as I can. I don't know how you might be trickin' me here with all this, but mark my words good—if it's all a lie, if you drug me into committing sin with deception, I'll take what blame I have comin' to make sure you get justice. We understood?"

A respect for the blacksmith prevented Josh from laughing at the man. Donegan had been through a lot. Most folks in town knew he had drank and laid with whores plenty until a few months ago. No one knew why he suddenly changed his ways, and Josh figured now was not the right time to ask.

"I understand," Josh said. "And it's no trick, I swear. Sometimes I wish to God it was."

Donegan gave a quick nod. "All right then, let's get this done."

WHEN THEY REACHED THE BANK, Josh stopped outside the door and turned to Donegan. The blacksmith's eyes were haunted, and his normally ruddy face was pale beneath the soot and dirt.

"You've seen what's become of the people of our town," Josh said. "Now, the decision is yours. We need your help, especially now. Are you with us?"

Donegan ran a hand over his face, smearing the dirt. "You convinced me. I already took part in murderin' folks. Robbin' the bank's goin' to be the least of my worries."

Josh let out a breath. His entire plan had been built on Donegan's participation. "Good. Let's go inside and see what we find."

Glory and Beatrice looked up from where they had been searching desk drawers behind the counter. Both women appeared to be on edge, and Glory held a pistol in her hand.

"What's wrong?" Josh asked.

"A wolf was waiting," Glory said, waving the pistol toward the securely locked safe.

Josh stepped up to the counter and peered over it at the wolf's body lying on the floor. He looked at Glory. "Do you think Balthazar left it here to stand guard?"

She set the pistol on the desk. "Wouldn't surprise me. It caught us off guard, nearly bit Beatrice."

"Wolves sitting in wait?" Donegan whispered, his eyes wide.

Josh knew he had to keep Donegan grounded. "Let's split up and look again. Maybe there's a note or something with the safe's combination. We need to hurry, the sun's high."

Half an hour later, they came together once again in front of the safe, all of them empty-handed. Josh dragged the wolf carcass out into the street.

"Looks like we can't get in the safe," Glory said. Sweat dampened her brow and upper lip.

"Shit." Josh stomped his foot and turned in a circle. "Well, I'm out of ideas."

Donegan squinted at the safe, blinked rapidly as sweat ran into his eye, and then he cleared his throat. "Lots of times I stood here in line staring at that door as I waited to deposit my money."

"Yeah?" Josh snapped. "Well, staring at it doesn't get it open, does it?"

"Hush," Beatrice said to him, and Josh pressed his lips together. He watched her take a step toward the blacksmith, softening her tone as she asked, "What'd you think about when you did that?"

Donegan flicked his gaze between the three of them before coming to rest on Beatrice. "I'd know it was wrong, but standing here staring at all those bags of money...." He gave an embarrassed, guilt-ridden shrug. "I'd think about how easy that door would blow with just one stick of dynamite."

"Sweet Christ," Josh gasped as a cold shiver rattled up his spine. "Dynamite's very unstable."

"I've heard horror stories about dynamite in the bar," Glory said. "It can go off in a man's hand and take his whole arm."

"I've used it," Donegan said in a choked whisper. "I used it in the war. I know how to handle it. Just one stick would do it. Those hinges ain't built too thick."

Josh looked at the safe, let his gaze touch on the hinges. He knew nothing about working with metal or dynamite, so he'd have to take Donegan's word for how easy it would be. His belly cramped with fear at the thought of having to handle even one stick of dynamite. But what other choice did they have? Where would they even find it?

He wished Dex was there with them. His wish was so strong that it felt, for the length of a breath, that Dex was indeed standing just behind his shoulder. That feeling of connection wove through him so sure and true, he almost turned his head to look over his shoulder, expecting to find Dex standing there as if he had never been taken.

But then the feeling vanished, and though it left Josh with a sure feeling that Dex was still alive, he also felt a deep sense of apprehension. Dex was in pain; Josh had felt the echoes like ghostly aches throughout his own body. Based on the hint of pain in his neck, he was afraid Dex may have been bitten. They had to get inside the safe, and soon. Dex was running out of time.

"All right, let's blow it," Josh said. "But where do we find dynamite? We don't have time to ride out to the mine and back before dark." And he wasn't sure he wanted to go back to that mine and see the bodies of those miners that had stood up from where they'd died, all because of him.

"General store," Donegan said. "There's a box of it in the back room."

"All right. Let's you and I go get it. Glory and Beatrice, stay here and keep looking for a combination written down."

As he followed Donegan along the boardwalk to the general store, Josh tried to get back the feeling that Dex was with him, but it was no use. It had been a powerful feeling, but short lived, and he had to hope Dex was still alive. That he was still human.

The box was in the back room of the store as Donegan had said, secured with a padlock. Without a word, Donegan tromped back into the main room of the store, returning a moment later with a crowbar.

"Careful," Josh couldn't help saying.

"Yup," Donegan replied before jamming the bar into the arms of the lock. He leaned on the curved handle, and the box shifted with his weight, scraping across the wood floor.

Josh's belly trembled at the sound, sure the entire box would blow up and scatter pieces of them both across the town.

With a quiet squeal of metal, the lock popped open. Donegan tossed the crowbar aside and worked the lock from the hasp. He lifted the lid, and they stood and stared at the red sticks packed in straw and lined up in rows.

"Christ," Josh whispered. "Be careful."

"Yup," Donegan said again, then he reached in to pluck out one of the sticks. He straightened up and looked at Josh, a shimmer of mad thrill in his eyes as he gave him a half smile. "I been wantin' to do this all my life."

Josh couldn't help smiling back. "Then let's go do it."

Glory and Beatrice turned when they walked back into the bank. "Did you find it?" Glory asked.

Donegan held up the dynamite. "Got it."

Glory and Beatrice backed away from the safe, gathering with Josh by the door. Quiet and breathless, they all watched as Donegan carefully balanced the stick of dynamite on the lower hinge. He turned and nodded to them, then pulled a box of matchsticks from his pocket. Josh jumped at the hiss and flare of the match, holding his breath as he watched Donegan touch the flame to the fuse, and then turned to push out of the bank and jump off the boardwalk as Donegan ran out after them.

The explosion blew out the windows of the bank and the general store next door. It blew off Josh's hat, and he felt the shards of glass fall across his back. When it was over, they slowly stood up and looked through the busted window to where the safe door hung suspended by the top hinge. Then Josh looked at each of the others in turn and, finally, they all let out wild whoops of laughter.

It felt good to laugh again. It had been so long since Josh had been able to laugh about anything, and the release of nervousness leading up to the detonation seemed to crack through the fear stored up inside him.

Beatrice looked around, her laughter fading as she peered up and down the empty street. As Donegan and Glory climbed the steps and dashed into the bank, Beatrice turned to Josh and said in a quiet voice, "No one's runnin' to see what that blast was all about. Guess we is all on our own then, ain't we?"

Josh's mood grew more somber, and he squeezed Beatrice's upper arm. "We can't let him get to any other towns, Bea. You see that, don't you?"

"I do."

"It worked!" Donegan shouted through the broken glass, and Josh heard Glory laugh again. "We can get inside!"

Josh tipped his head toward the door, and he and Beatrice hurried into the bank where they joined Glory and Donegan in front of the safe. The door hung askew, held by only the top hinge that the explosion had twisted out of true. A space gaped at the far bottom corner, dark and inviting, and they eased the door open wider so Josh could crawl inside.

The interior was dark as pitch and cool, smelling of copper and musty paper. He paused a moment to take a breath, realizing just how far outside the law he had now traveled. He could never go back to where he had started; everything about his life had changed.

A yellow light flickered at the opening and Donegan stretched in his arm to hand over a candle. The big man paused with his face pressed to the gap, his body too thick to squeeze into the safe.

"How much is there do you think?" Donegan asked in an awed whisper.

"A lot," Josh replied as he held up the candle and inspected the cash, notes, and coins stacked on shelves. "Quite a lot."

Donegan lowered his voice even more. "How much you gonna take?"

"Just the silver," Josh said. "Nothing else." He looked down at Donegan's face, the candle flame exposing the greed in his eyes. "Donegan." The man blinked and looked up at him. "Get your wagon from the smithy. We'll load the bags of silver in it."

Donegan looked from Josh to the stacks of money and back again. Then he pressed his lips together, nodded once, and moved away from the gap. Josh got on his hands and knees and looked out through the gap at Glory and Beatrice. "Think you can find another wagon we can use to get the coal?"

Beatrice grinned and touched the brim of her leather hat. "You can count on us. Let's go, Glory."

Josh watched the women hurry out of the bank, then got to his feet, hefting a bag of silver in each hand. He set them by the gap in the door and fetched two more, thinking that maybe their luck had changed. He didn't want to get too comfortable and let down his guard, but they just might stand a chance.

Sometime later, when Josh and Donegan had two dozen bags of silver coins loaded, they heard the sound of a wagon approaching. Josh stood in the back of the blacksmith's wagon, Donegan in the front, reins held loose in one big hand, shading his eyes with the other as he stared down the road.

"That them?" Donegan asked, voice shaky with nerves. "It's them, right?"

Josh squinted at the approaching wagon. "Yup. It's them."

Moments later, the wagon pulled even with the bank and came to a stop. Glory and Beatrice rode in the front, both grinning. Josh couldn't help grinning back.

"Where'd you find this?" he asked as he climbed from Donegan's wagon into the back of the new one.

"General store," Beatrice said. "Sittin' right out back."

"Wait," Donegan practically shouted. "Where you goin'?"

"We need to get the coal," Josh told him. "It'll be dark soon. The more of us there are, the faster it'll be. Take the silver back to the shop and unload it, then lock up tight. If it ain't us knocking, don't open up."

"You gonna leave me with all this silver we stole?" Donegan said, waving at the heavy bags stacked in the back of his wagon.

"If the Sheriff does come around, stolen silver is the least of your worries," Glory said. "He'll be wanting to drain your blood."

Beatrice snapped the reins, and the horses took off at a fast clip. She turned to look back at Josh and said with a grin, "Best hold tight."

CHAPTER

NINE

Josh sat in the back of the wagon and held on as it bumped along the road. Beatrice drove the horses hard, and Glory sat beside her, holding tight to the seat back. By the angle of the sun, Josh knew it was well past noon. It had taken more time than he had anticipated convincing Donegan to help them, and then even longer getting into the safe. He hoped the coal would be easier. It had to be easier.

Josh was tired, and he closed his eyes. The rocking of the wagon, rough and unsteady though it was, felt soothing to him, and he took advantage of the chance to sit back and ride for a change rather than lead.

With some time to shift his thoughts away from immediate danger and planning, Josh turned them to Dex. That feeling of Dex being near came over him again, and it helped to still the shaky nervousness inside his chest. It was as if Dex sat right there in the wagon beside him, leg pressed against Josh's, his dark hair hanging down over his forehead, and his blue eyes fixed on Josh's face.

Dull, distant anxiety tightened Josh's chest, and those

ghostly aches flared again in his neck and right forearm. It wasn't the fear and pain directly, but the suggestion of it. His skin rippled with gooseflesh at the thought. He had established a connection with Dex, he could feel it. Dex was scared and injured, bitten by Balthazar, and Josh had picked up on those feelings.

Keeping his eyes shut tight, Josh thought about some of the good times they had shared, sifted through memories of their years of friendship. The ghostly anxiety in his chest lessened a little, and a shard of hope glittered within him. He knew, without any doubt, that he had gotten a fix on Dex and had been able to connect with him. And, hopefully, his calming thoughts had helped to soothe Dex's fear.

But the pain in his neck worried him. Josh had to believe that Dex had been bitten, but how many times? He reasoned that if he could still establish some kind of connection with Dex, he had not been turned. Yet.

"Coming for you," Josh whispered, and he pushed the thought out to Dex, hoping that words as well as emotions could cross the cruel lands of Venom Valley. "Soon. Hold on."

A particularly jarring bump lifted Josh's ass up off the wagon and brought his eyes open. He lost the connection he had with Dex, and he pounded the side of his fist against the floor of the wagon in frustration. Another bump made him flinch, and he shifted position, moving away from the wagon's sides to avoid scraping his back when they went over bumps. A quilt lay folded in the front corner and he laid down, resting his head on it as he stretched out on his back. It was soft and made of patches of old material, just like the dusty quilt which he and Dex had spread beneath them when they had first made love. They had pulled it from the bed in the house where Josh had been raised until the night his mother vanished.

Josh stared up at the white clouds a moment, then closed his eyes and tried once more to reach out to Dex. He let his mind go as he worked to find that feeling again, that connection, but he couldn't do it. Dex's mind was beyond his reach now, and Josh hoped it didn't mean he had been hurt even more. Or worse.

A loneliness opened inside him, a yearning to have Dex with him once again. They had often gone days without seeing each other, but things were different now. He missed being able to talk with Dex, look at him, touch him. This yearning brought back memories of their time together, of the night they'd spent taking refuge in the small cabin crouched on the edge of Venom Valley. The night they had pronounced their love for each other.

Had he really, truly lain with Dex? Touched him as no other had before? Had the man stretched out naked beside him, braced himself above Josh, and pushed his length into him?

Josh remembered how Dex had kissed him once, then again, and a comforting warmth spread through him, pushing back the chill of loneliness. Dex had moved lower after those kisses to take him in his mouth. The memory of Dex's mouth on him, hot and eternal around his cock, coaxing the come out of him, made Josh hard all over again.

Josh had quickly returned the favor, licking Dex, tasting him, sucking his cock and swallowing the thick warm semen when he came. Desire pent up over the years of their friendship had them ready again in minutes, and Josh had laid back and opened himself to Dex. The man had taken his time, first running his tongue over the tight wrinkled hole, and then slipping in a finger to push his spit deep. Dex's cock had followed, easing in and stretching Josh open, wedging himself deep inside where no one had ever touched him before. Dex had taken care to move slowly, to push in and pull back steadily, until he fucked Josh fast and deep.

They had told each other "I love you," as Dex moved inside Josh, and moments later Josh's second climax spiraled up and out of him, coating his sweaty torso with come. Dex had come soon after, still inside him, supported above Josh as he caught his breath and leaned down for another kiss.

The wagon hit a hard bump and jolted Josh from his memories. He opened his eyes and looked up, watching Beatrice haul back on the reins to slow the horses. Josh sat up and looked around. They were just west of the Belkin's Pass train station, a small clapboard building that rose out of the flat prairie land like a stubborn stone. Nearby stood a covered, fenced off area piled high with coal.

"Here it is," Beatrice said. She brought the horses to a stop, and they climbed down to stand and look at the pile of coal twice their height.

"That's a lot of coal," Glory said.

Beatrice nodded. "Yup. Sharp corners, too. Don't think I didn't learn that lesson quick." She adjusted her hat, threw a squint-eyed glare at the sun sitting lower in the sky, then stomped over to grab some flat-edged shovels that leaned against the wall of the coal bin. "Best get a move on. Losing sun."

They got to work, bending, scooping, and turning to toss the coal into the wagon. The horses snorted and stomped nervously when the first loads of hard coal hit the wood floor, but they settled soon after. In a short time, Josh's shirt was soaked with sweat and stained nearly black from coal dust. It coated his hands, and he felt it sticking to the sweat on his face as well.

The rhythm of the work lulled them all into a dream-like state. Josh's back muscles tightened at the unfamiliar motions, and he figured Beatrice and Glory felt it even worse. Finally, they'd filled the wagon so high that rocks of coal began to roll over the sides. Beatrice stopped to straighten up, putting a hand to her back and wincing.

"Cain't fit in no more," Beatrice said. She tipped back her hat and dragged a sleeve across her face, smearing it black. "Just like some of the men I used to see back at the Rooster."

A chuckle from somewhere inside him surprised Josh, and he noticed that even Glory laughed and shook her head. Josh turned to look at the sun, and his humor was swiftly overtaken by fear.

"Sun's going down fast," he said, and tossed the shovel back into the bin. "We gotta go."

"We'll take two shovels with us," Beatrice said. "Gotta be able to unload it, too."

Josh nodded and shot another worried glance at the lowering sun. "Good idea. Let's go."

He let Glory go ahead of him up into the seat, and then climbed up himself. Glory sat between Josh and Beatrice, and he was glad to see she held a rifle across her lap. He had left Dex's revolver back at the smithy. At least one of them had been thinking about protecting themselves.

"Hold tight," Beatrice said as she picked up the reins. "We gotta ride fast to beat the sun set."

Josh looked around, a sense of unease growing within him. The shadows seemed to lengthen even as he watched.

"Hiyah!" Beatrice snapped the reins, and the horses started forward, straining to pull the heavy load.

"Is it too much for 'em?" Josh asked.

"Can't right say yet," Beatrice replied. "They're tryin' to get it goin'."

The horses finally found traction, and the wagon rolled slowly forward. Josh looked over his shoulder to where the sun was sinking fast behind the mountains that ringed Venom Valley.

"Gotta go faster," he shouted. A few coal rocks tumbled down into the front of the wagon. One bumped over the backrest and onto the seat. The sharp edges snagged Josh's trouser leg, tearing a hole and nicking the skin beneath. He cursed under his breath and dropped the rock onto the floor at his feet.

"Goin' fast as we can," Beatrice replied.

"We're going to be close," Glory said.

"Not goin' to make it," Josh mumbled, meeting her frightened gaze.

As if in answer, a long, mournful wolf howl echoed across the prairie. The sound of it sent a shiver down Josh's back, and he realized they only had one gun to protect them. All he had was the cross bouncing against his skin beneath his shirt.

"We're in trouble," Glory said.

TEN

The wolves came up on them fast.

Josh leaned out of the side of the wagon to look around the pile of coal and watched them approach across the flat prairie, heads down and tails straight back. He didn't think Balthazar controlled them as it was still daylight, but it didn't make them any less terrifying.

"Wolves!" Josh shouted.

Glory turned her head back and forth, trying to see around the coal. "Where?"

Josh pointed out his side of the wagon. "Give me the rifle!"

Instead of handing him the rifle, she got to her feet, knelt precariously on the bench, and looked behind them. Josh reached out to keep her steady, but stayed his hand just before he touched her hip. As much as they had been through together, propriety kept him from touching her. Instead, he turned to watch her take aim behind them, ready to reach out and grab hold of her if she should fall backward. As he watched the barrel of the rifle, he realized he was holding his breath. When she finally let off the shot, he exhaled and leaned out to look behind. Still two wolves, but the gunshot had startled them so that they had lost some ground.

But not for long. Faster than Josh expected, the two wolves closed on them. Soon they were trailing the wagon by a very short distance. A jarring bump brought another rock of coal clattering down onto the seat. Josh picked it up and hefted it in his hand to feel the weight. He'd always been able to throw rocks with a good eye. If the wolves got closer, he could hit them. He closed his fingers around the sharp edges and turned to watch. The wolves gained ground, and Josh pulled back his arm. The way he was positioned, he was forced to use his left arm instead of his right, so he waited until he felt he had a clear shot, then threw the rock as hard as he could. The coal missed the wolf, bouncing off the hard packed dirt to its left.

"Dammit!" Josh turned around and reached for another rock. When he looked back, he was surprised to find the wolves even closer. Had the horses slowed down or the wolves put on speed?

"They're catching up!" Josh shouted.

"Horses are tiring," Beatrice shouted back.

Glory was still on her feet and took another shot, then cursed and dropped into the seat beside him. Josh looked back at her and watched as she worked the bolt.

"What's wrong?" he asked.

"Jammed!"

"We need it," he told her.

"I know!" Glory shouted back without looking up at him.

Josh leaned out the side of the wagon again, his arm cocked for another throw. He focused on the larger wolf on the right, kept his attention trained on it, hoping to send the piece of coal right at it. A moment before he threw, a gunshot cracked through the orange evening light. Josh jumped and watched as the wolf went down in a tumbling blur of tail and legs.

That shot had definitely not come from Glory. It had come from somewhere off to the side.

Another shot brought down the second wolf. Josh was able to pinpoint the shooter's location by the muzzle flash. There were two of them, actually, and when he squinted against the setting sun, he thought they might be dressed in the dark uniforms of the US Army. The strangers rode sleek, fast warhorses, and they fell in behind to follow them back into town.

"Who is that?" Glory asked him.

Josh turned to face her. "I don't know. They look like Army."

"Army?" Beatrice said. "We in trouble?"

"Not yet," Josh replied, and he turned to look at the men behind them.

As they entered the town limits, the riders trailing them pulled off and disappeared from view. Josh watched them go with a frown, then looked ahead to see Donegan throw open the doors to the blacksmith shop at the sound of their approach. Beatrice guided the horses inside, and Josh jumped off the wagon when they stopped. A few new arrivals, three men, three women, and a young girl, stood around watching nervously. Josh looked them over quickly, noted blood spatters on some of their clothing and the wide-eyed look of shock on a couple of faces. These people had been through a lot.

He stood at the doors to the street to await their saviors, and Beatrice and Glory joined him.

"Y'all look a right mess," Donegan said, his voice a thick, wet rumble.

"Shovelin' coal will do that to a lady," Beatrice replied, nodding to the new group. "Where'd you find these folks?"

Donegan shrugged and scuffed the toe of his boot into the dirt floor. "Saw a few wandering down the street, convinced them to join us. They told me about the others and I rode out to get 'em." Donegan shot a glance at Josh. "Figured it was the least I could do after what else I done today."

Josh nodded to the blacksmith, then noticed Beatrice's smile. Even through the dirt and coal dust, it helped her round face look pretty as she said, "That was right nice a' you."

"Weren't nothin'," Donegan mumbled, then he stepped up to the doors.

The blacksmith was about to take a step over the threshold, but Josh put a hand on his arm to hold him back. "Not beyond the threshold. Not this close to sundown."

"Why's that?" Donegan asked.

"Vampires can't cross a threshold unless invited," Glory said. "You're safe inside."

Donegan peered nervously out at the darkness taking over the street. "Why we still got the doors open then?"

"Some men in Army uniforms followed us into town," Josh said. "They shot a couple wolves trying to run us down, but turned off as we got into the Pass. I'm waiting to see if they show up."

"Think they'll arrest us for stealing coal?" Beatrice asked.

"Arrest us?" Donegan swallowed nervously and pulled one of the heavy wood doors shut, the smell of his sweat drifting over Josh. "I don't see no one. I'm closin' up." Donegan crossed and pulled the other door shut, closing them inside the smithy. He leaned closer to Josh and lowered his voice. "We stole bags of silver from the bank, and before that we put stakes in the hearts of people in this town. We cain't let them in here with all that silver sittin' there." Donegan dragged a hand down his face. "They was Army you said?"

"I think so." Josh turned to Glory and Beatrice. "Did either of you get a look at them?"

Both women shook their heads. "Never even saw 'em," Glory said. "Just heard the shots."

"Me neither," Beatrice said. "I was too busy keepin' the horses at a run."

Beatrice and Glory turned to the horses still harnessed to the wagon full of coal and backed them up closer to the forge. They unhitched the horses and led them to the last two stalls in the back corner, alongside Clementine and Nightshade. Josh and Donegan arranged the bags of coins near the forge and shoveled loads of coal from the wagon into the bin nearby. Two of the men who were new arrivals grabbed shovels from Donegan's tool rack and came over to help.

"You ever burn coal in this?" Josh asked, running a hand over the rough surface of the stone forge.

"Once," Donegan said with a nod. "Not hot enough to melt silver, mind you, but I had some tough iron needed melting for the railroad. It's gonna heat up in here real quick."

A pounding startled them all, and they turned to stare at the heavy wooden doors.

"Is it them?" Donegan whispered. "Is it them vampires?"

"They don't usually knock," Josh replied, his voice low.

"Can't be wolves," Glory said from across the room.

Josh glanced her way and saw the strange yellow glow pulsing around her. He decided that it must be some form of protective Indian magic. If so, they might truly be in trouble.

He turned back to the door, took a breath, and called out, "Who's there?"

"Sergeant Walker Maxwell, 8th Cavalry," a gruff voice responded. "I demand entrance by order of the United States Army."

"It is the Army," Beatrice said. "Think they're from Fort Emmerick?"

"Closest fort around these parts," Josh replied. "That'd make the most sense. But why the devil are they here in Belkin's Pass?" He looked around, his gaze touching on each frightened face. He put his hands on his hips and looked down at the dirt floor, lips pressed tight as he contemplated his choices.

"As a representative of the military, I demand that you open up!" the man shouted, pounding hard on the door.

"Josh?" Glory said, her eyes wide. "We can't leave them out there. Sun's almost down."

Josh waved a hand at her. "I know. Dammit." He looked at the bags of stolen silver coins and piles of coal. This was going to be very difficult to explain to an outsider.

At that moment, one of the men outside the door let out a bark of surprise, and Josh heard him say to his partner, "Did you hear that?"

One of the horses in the stalls stamped its feet and snorted nervously.

Josh shook his head before stooping to grab a handful of coins. He wanted something silver in his hands in case he met a vampire. "Everyone stay calm. I'm going to let them inside." He held the coins tight in one sweaty fist and moved to the door. The lock resisted his efforts at first, but finally disengaged, allowing Josh to pull the door open a few feet.

Two men stepped inside, one tall and broad shouldered, handsome in a dark, authoritative manner. The other man was shorter, heavy in the stomach, with curly hair and fair skin. Prairie dust coated the taller man's dark blue Army uniform, and the yellow insignia on his sleeve that signified he was a sergeant was darkened with dirt. A pair of mutton chops grew down the sides of his face, dark and thick, coming to straight-edged ends at the corners of his mouth. His dark-eyed gaze moved quickly over all of them, then came back to Josh.

"Who is the owner of this smithy?" the sergeant asked, narrowing his eyes with suspicion.

Donegan stepped forward, eyes wide and voice shaking when he said, "I... I am, sir."

The sergeant moved to stand directly in front of Donegan. "I am placing you under arrest."

"What?" Donegan's normally deep voice rose in pitch with his fear and surprise. He darted a terrified glance toward Josh before looking back at the sergeant. "For what charge?"

"From the looks of it, a number of them," the man said. "Stealing coal from the train depot, for one. That's a federal crime as the rail system falls under the federal government." Maxwell stepped around Donegan and crouched down to grab a handful of coins from an open bag, jingling them in his glove-covered palm a moment before looking up at him. "I wouldn't expect a blacksmith to have this much silver lying around."

"The crimes are not his," Josh said, and took a step forward. "If any of us here is guilty of a crime, I am."

The sergeant stood, gripping the coins in his hand, and walked up to Josh. His dark, narrowed eyes glittered in the lamplight, and his full lips pursed as he studied Josh.

"Your name?"

"Joshua Stanton."

"So be it. Joshua Stanton, I hereby arrest you for the crimes of theft and bank robbery." Maxwell looked at the man who had entered behind him. "Private Hicks, secure the prisoner."

The heavyset man reached in a bag slung around his shoulders and withdrew a set of wrist binders. He glared at Josh and said, "Hands in front."

Josh dropped the coins he held, hearing them clink together as they hit the dirt floor, and put his hands together before him. He turned to look at Sergeant Maxwell.

"You can't take me outside."

"Oh?" Sergeant Maxwell raised his eyebrows. "I'm not used to my prisoners telling me what I can and can't do."

Josh tipped his head toward the door. "There will be a whole pack of wolves out there waiting for us, just like the ones you saved us from out on the road."

"Not just wolves neither," Beatrice said.

Maxwell turned to look Glory, Beatrice, and Donegan over, and then shifted his gaze to inspect the other survivors before bringing his attention back to Josh. "As my prisoner, you will be taken to the local sheriff's office and secured in a cell until formal charges can be brought against you."

"The sheriff is dead," Glory said.

Maxwell and Hicks shared a look before the sergeant crossed the room to stand before Glory, looming above her. Josh had to give her credit. Glory stood her ground and stared up at the man, hands on hips.

"Then the deputy will take him into custody," Maxwell said.

"He's dead, too." Glory raised her eyebrows. "And the other deputy is missing."

Maxwell looked back at Josh. "What the devil is going on in this town?"

Josh nodded. "That's about right."

Maxwell frowned. "What's that mean?"

"The devil is taking over this town," Josh said. "His name is Balthazar. He has turned half of the town into night walking, blood-drinking demons like himself, and used the other half for food."

"Lord," Hicks whispered, his breath smelling of onion and dried beef as it washed over Josh. "Demons?"

"Dammit, Hicks," Maxwell snapped. "He's just telling stories."

"It ain't stories," a man from the group of new arrivals said as he stepped forward. "I seen it." He waved a hand to the others standing around him. "We all seen it. We all lost family to 'em. The wolves and the demons."

A wolf howl from just outside the doors rose the hairs on the back of Josh's neck, and everyone turned to look in that direction.

Josh looked at Maxwell and said, "They're here."

CHAPTER

ELEVEN

The terrified cries of the horses outside took both Army men to the door.

"No!" Josh shouted, reaching out for them with his bound hands. "They'll kill you!"

Maxwell ignored Josh. He drew his Colt revolver then pulled open one door a couple of feet. Josh backed away to stand with Glory and Beatrice, the metal binders tight around his wrists as he helplessly watched the men step outside.

"What about vampires?" Glory asked. "They can't be far from the wolves."

"Quick, grab some silver coins," Josh said. "If there are vampires out there, the coins will burn them."

Glory and Beatrice hurried across the room, passing Donegan and the other survivors who had all moved to stand against the back wall. The group stared at the doors with wide eyes, faces pale and drawn tight with tension.

"Donegan!" Josh shouted. The blacksmith blinked and

looked over at him. Josh held up his wrists. "Get me out of these bindings."

"But, the sergeant..." Donegan began.

"He's in trouble!" Josh snapped. "He's going to need our help, and I can't do anything with these on."

Snarls and a yelp erupted outside, followed by squeals from the horses. Josh turned away from Donegan who pressed himself even more firmly against the back wall. Moving quickly, Josh crossed to the door and stood off to one side. Glory and Beatrice moved up beside him, their hands full of silver coins.

"I ain't held this much money in my hands in all my life," Beatrice whispered.

"Hush," Josh snapped. The bindings on his wrists made him feel useless, and he could hear the edge it gave to his voice as they stood just inside the threshold and peered out the door. An apron of lantern light pushed the night back a dozen feet, stretching their shadows out before them.

Josh leaned farther out from behind the doorframe and then froze. A pack of wolves crouched in the shadows just outside the reach of the light, the sight of them and their number sending a cold shock of dread through him. The pack had doubled in size, and they all looked hungry. Maxwell and Hicks had their backs turned to the pack, each man holding a revolver in one hand as he struggled to untie his horse from the post with the other.

A wolf in the front, his muzzle painted gold by lamplight, hunkered down and crept closer to the men.

"Watch out!" Josh shouted.

Maxwell half-turned his head, saw the approaching wolf, then saw the pack. His eyes widened, and he looked back at Josh, accusation and anger mingling in his gaze. Instead of firing at the approaching wolf, Maxwell narrowed his eyes and lifted a corner of his upper lip to snarl at the beast. The sound carried through the night to Josh, deep, foreboding, and arousing in a purely animal way. A flicker of something dark and hot sparked low in Josh's belly even as the creeping wolf halted in its tracks.

A tall shadow behind the wolves shifted and in the space of a breath, a man stood beside the Army men. In the lamplight, Josh saw Langstrom McBriddle, the owner of the general store.

Before any of them could call out a warning, Langstrom came up behind Hicks and grabbed a handful of his hair. He pulled Hicks's head back and to the side, exposing his throat, then bit into the flesh where it joined with Hicks's shoulder. Hicks screamed and blood spilled out of his mouth, running down the front of his Army uniform. His arms flailed, and his left foot kicked the air before him. Hicks's wide eyes darted wildly until they finally rolled to white. Drawn by the scent of blood, the wolves advanced, heads lowered, tongues hanging out. They snapped at one another and a few snagged the material of Hicks's pants, tugging to try and pull the body free. Langstrom kicked at them, sending some yelping back into the night as he gorged on Hicks's blood.

Maxwell loosed his horse and gave a shout of surprise. The horse stormed past Josh, Glory, and Beatrice into the smithy where one of the men near the back caught the reins and tried to calm the animal. Maxwell aimed his revolver into the air and fired twice, then shouted, "Leave him!"

The wolves retreated out of the light, but Langstrom did not even flinch.

"Silver!" Josh shouted. "Use the silver."

"Here!" Glory threw the coins she held, and they fell around Maxwell's booted feet.

The sergeant picked up a coin and advanced on Langstrom. Maxwell pressed the coin against Langstrom's cheek and even from where he stood, Josh could hear the sizzle and pop as the skin burned. The vampire pulled away, tearing wide the flesh and artery in Hicks's neck. A stream of blood arced from Hicks's wound to spatter into the dirt as the vampire screamed, the sound piercing and terrifying. In a flash, it vanished into the night.

Maxwell barely managed to catch Hicks's heavy body before it hit the ground. He sagged under the dead weight and staggered as he tried to keep the man up while keeping his grip on his weapon.

"Inside!" Beatrice called. "Bring him inside!"

Maxwell dragged Hicks into the smithy, and Glory and Beatrice bolted the doors just in time to keep the wolves outside. Laying Hicks on the dirt floor, Maxwell stared into the private's wide eyes and pulled off his gloves to press a hand to the ragged flesh of his neck in an effort to staunch the blood.

"Speak to me, Hicks," Maxwell commanded. "Don't you leave me, now. Talk to me. Who's your best girl back home?"

Josh saw Hicks's lips move, but no sound came out. A thick runner of blood bubbled as he drew his last breath.

Maxwell pressed harder against the wound, his jaw tightening beneath his mutton chops. "Private Hicks! I am your sergeant, and I command you to respond to me! Private Hicks!"

"He's gone," Glory said. She reached down to touch Maxwell's shoulder, but the man swatted her hand away and got to his feet.

"You are all under arrest!" Maxwell shouted. When he turned, Josh could see rage and loss burning in Maxwell's dark eyes. "I will start with you first. But mark my words, each of you will be arrested and held accountable for this man's death."

Warm nausea surged through Josh, and he closed his eyes. He staggered back a few steps, feeling the chain of the binders swing with the motion.

"Josh?" Glory's voice sounded as if she stood across the room instead of a few feet away. "What is it?"

The familiar heat blazed to life inside him, stretching fingers of fire through his limbs. Sweat trickled down his face and back. He could feel it gathering on the palms of his hands and bottoms of his feet as he backed away from Hicks's body.

"Stay where you are," Maxwell said.

Josh looked up at the man, locked his gaze on Maxwell's, and said, "You have to get that body out of here. Now."

Maxwell stared at him in surprised shock. "Out to the wolves? And that flesh-eating man?"

"It was no man," Glory said.

Maxwell turned to glare at her. "He walked on two legs like a man."

"Vampire," Beatrice said. "Not living and not dead. Three bites from one a'em and you become 'em, unless they just drink all your blood. I seen it happen to the girls we worked with at the Rooster. And now most of the town."

Maxwell looked between them, and when a hot cramp stitched into Josh's side and dropped him to his knees, the sergeant took a step toward him before stopping himself.

"What trickery is this?" Maxwell demanded.

"Get the body out of here," Josh said. "It's... it's making me sick."

"He gave his life protecting the lot of you," Maxwell said, glaring at each of them in turn. "And now you're demanding I throw his body outside to be ravaged by wolves?"

As if called by Maxwell's words, wicked snarls erupted outside the heavy doors and Hicks's horse let out a terrified whinny. The sounds of the horse's hooves stamping the ground came to them through the doors, then the heavy thud of the animal hitting the ground. Growls and yelps followed as the wolves descended on the horse, and Josh watched through bleary eyes as the sergeant's jaw tightened. Maxwell reached into a leather pouch on his belt and produced a handful of bullets he loaded into his Colt as he crossed to the doors.

"If it's a fight they want, that's what they'll get." Maxwell snapped the Colt's cylinder closed and reached for the latch.

"No!" Josh, Glory, Beatrice, and Donegan all screamed at once.

But it was too late. Maxwell pulled open one half of the double doors. A wolf jumped at him, and he shot it out of the air. The horses inside the smithy reared up, braying and rolling their eyes, and men ran to try and soothe them. A number of wolves had their muzzles buried in the belly of Hicks's horse, and they looked up at the sound of the gunshot, bloodstained lips drawn back from their teeth. Two more wolves stepped into the light and over the threshold where they stopped, bared fangs reflecting back the lamplight.

Maxwell took aim, but before he could pull the trigger, the two wolves ducked their heads, whined, and turned to run off into the night. The wolves feasting on the horse lifted their heads to scent the wind, whined as well, and fled with their tails between their legs. The howls and yips that had filled the cool night air fell silent, and Maxwell glanced over his shoulder at Josh.

"They left," Maxwell said. "I'll be damned."

"Means something worse is comin'," Donegan said in a quiet voice.

Josh closed his eyes as he struggled to contain the power building within him. He could feel it clawing at the inside of his skin, trying to get out. It pushed against the inner walls of his body and reached out to Hicks's corpse, hungry to make it move yet again.

"Oh, sergeant," a deep, smooth voice rolled out of the darkness. "You are not damned. Not yet."

Josh opened his eyes and saw the tall shape of Balthazar standing just outside the threshold. The vampire's face gleamed in the flickering lamplight, pale and shadowed like a small moon, the mark of Josh's cross burned into his cheek. His eyes, sunk deep beneath his heavy brow, gleamed red as bloody embers.

"Come closer, sergeant," Balthazar coaxed. "Let me whisper secrets in your ear."

Balthazar's red-eyed gaze caught Maxwell's and held it fast. Josh watched as the sergeant lowered his revolver and took a reluctant step toward the door.

"No!" Josh shouted, his voice ragged with the effort it took for him to keep Hicks's corpse from rising. "Stop him!"

Glory crossed the open shop, fists clenched. Josh watched her move, saw the yellow glow of her protection flare into life. As he watched, Glory ran up beside Maxwell and pulled back her fist. She let it fly and clipped the sergeant on the chin, spinning him away from Balthazar and breaking their eye contact.

The vampire hissed and raised a hand to point a long, wickedly sharp nail at her. "Your spirit can't protect you forever, half-breed whore. And when he tires of you, rest assured I'll be nearby waiting to bend you to my will. Your lovely friend Edith has proven especially useful to me, and I know she'd be eager for you to join us. I've sent her on a special errand, otherwise she'd be here to tell you so herself."

Glory leaned toward the vampire, closing the distance between herself and Balthazar. Just when it seemed she would continue leaning forward right into his grasp, Glory stopped and spit on him.

And then Hicks's hand twitched.

Josh felt the corpse's movements as surely as if they were his own. He knelt on the floor, head hung low, sweat dripping onto the dirt floor. His physical exhaustion and inexperience dealing with the power hiding deep inside made him vulnerable to the proximity of Hicks's body. The power he tried so hard to contain broke through his mental blockade, sent heat rushing through him and reaching out to the dead man lying nearby. Josh lifted his head and watched wearily as Hicks's limbs jittered and slapped against the dirt floor.

"Hicks?" Maxwell said, moving toward the body.

"Stay back!" Josh shouted. The desperation in his voice stopped the sergeant in his tracks. "Don't go near him!"

Hicks sat up. His eyes opened, but they were clouded and vacant of life. Tendons creaked and popped, and the skin torn open by the vampire flapped and oozed blood as Hicks turned his head to look at Josh. Hicks's mouth opened, and he let out a chilling moan.

TWELVE

"Hicks?" Sergeant Maxwell asked, his voice quiet and shaking.

"It's not Hicks," Glory said as she stepped back from the door and Balthazar. "Keep away from him."

Maxwell glared at her. "What do you mean it's not Hicks? He's right here." Maxwell approached the corpse and extended a hand toward him.

Hicks turned his head fast to snap at Maxwell. The sergeant jerked his hand away and took several steps back. His shock was apparent by the expression on his face, and Josh forced himself to look away from the living people in the room and focus on Hicks. Now that the body had risen, he needed to try and repeat what he had done with the miners when he had been with Dex. Much as he hated to do it, he needed to control Hicks, use the man's corpse to their advantage.

Josh closed his eyes and cleared his mind, focusing on a simple course of action. He pictured Hicks turning to the door and approaching Balthazar. But try as he might to connect with the thing across the room, Josh couldn't do it. The day's work had left him tired, and the struggle to contain the power of resurrection had sapped what little energy he had left. He opened his eyes and watched as Hicks struggled to his feet, his limbs stiff, and a low, wet moan rumbling in his ruined throat.

Hicks found his footing and stood upright, turning his vacant eyes to Sergeant Maxwell who stood closest to him. He took one shuffling step, and then another as he advanced on the man.

"He moves as if alive," Maxwell said in a low voice. "How can this be? I saw him die."

"He's dead," Glory assured him. "He's beyond our help now." She looked at Josh, her expression concerned and on the verge of fearful as she whispered, "Can you do it?"

Josh shook his head and tightened his lips. He closed his eyes and focused all his energy on trying to make a connection with Hicks.

"Dear God in Heaven above," Donegan said in a shaky voice. "What deviltry is this now?"

"I ain't seen a dead man get up and walk before," Beatrice said. "Who's tellin him to do it?"

No one spoke; all eyes were on Hicks as the private advanced on Maxwell.

"Hicks?" Maxwell said, his voice quiet and unsure.

Josh formed another image in his mind, this one of Hicks turning toward Balthazar. He made the vision as clear as possible and pushed the thought out to Hicks, but the corpse continued to stagger toward Maxwell.

"What is this?" Balthazar asked.

Josh could feel the vampire's gaze on him but refused to open his eyes. Instead, he took a deep breath, clenched his fists, squeezed his eyes even tighter, and conjured the scene in his mind. He pictured the inside of the smithy, saw where everyone stood, and set Hicks's stumbling corpse within that space. Then he changed the angle of Hicks's path in his mind, envisioned him approaching Balthazar instead of Maxwell, and pushed that thought out along the unsteady connection he felt with Hicks.

It worked. Josh could feel it. It felt similar to the bond he had made earlier with Dex, but this connection differed in a darker fashion. Hicks's body was hungry for this power. Drained of it by death, it craved what Josh sent to it. And the effort to keep that link in check sapped Josh's strength even faster.

If Dex were with him, supporting him, giving Josh his strength, it might be different. But Josh was alone, and his lack of sleep and physical exhaustion made the connection to Hicks fragile. The corpse took one last step toward Maxwell, stopped within arm's reach of the sergeant, then turned toward the open door. A shuddering step, and another after that took it toward Balthazar.

Josh could see the vampire's distorted outline through Hicks's clouded eyes. He felt the hunger for flesh that roared through Hicks's body. The dank, red feeling that pushed back into Josh from the connection mixed with the heat that boiled within him, and made him feel even more nauseous.

But he couldn't break the connection with Hicks. If he did that, the corpse would attack the rest of them, and only a bullet to the head would bring him down. And he didn't think Maxwell would be willing to shoot his partner in the head, walking dead or not.

"Are you doing this?" Balthazar's voice was cold and

hard. Through his connection with Hicks, Josh could see the vampire's eyes glow even brighter as he pointed at Josh.

"Josh?" Maxwell's voice was quiet, frightened. "What?"

Josh pushed Hicks another two feet then opened his own eyes and met Balthazar's red-eyed stare. "Leave us. Or die."

"You," Balthazar whispered, truly stunned by the revelation. "It is you. This is what I've been sensing about you."

"Leave us," Josh repeated. Hicks was three steps from the threshold. "Now."

Balthazar stood taller, his shoulders squared and powerful chest out. "You dare threaten me? I have walked this earth for centuries. More men have died and been turned by my hand than have ever lived in this dust blown town. Your feeble powers are no match for me. Let us see just how powerful your puppet really is."

With a nod of his head, Balthazar took a step back and Langstrom McBriddle appeared in his place. The black mark from the silver coin stood out against the smooth pale skin of his cheek.

"You!" Maxwell lifted his gun. "Murderer!" He fired at Langstrom until the hammer of his Colt clicked on empty cylinders. The vampire's shirt fluttered and holes appeared in the fabric, but the creature did not even flinch, just fixed his red-eyed stare on Maxwell and growled low in his throat.

"You're wasting bullets," Glory snapped. "Save them for the wolves."

Maxwell looked stunned as he holstered his gun. "What kind of beasts are these?"

Before anyone could respond to Maxwell, Hicks stepped across the threshold and Langstrom grabbed him by the shoulders. Josh squinted and had Hicks duck his head to bite into the vampire's arm. Hicks's teeth tore through the pale skin and crunched through bone. Black blood poured from the wound as Langstrom threw back his head and shrieked into the night sky. He took hold of both of Hicks's arms where they joined his shoulders and tore the limbs off, flinging them behind him into the night. Hicks lunged forward to bury his mouth into the flesh connecting the vampire's neck and shoulder and bit deep. A thick gout of black blood washed over the lower half of Hicks's face.

"Jesus save us," Beatrice whispered.

Josh ignored everyone around him, keeping his gaze locked on the figures in the doorway. Now that Hicks had found flesh to bite into, the risen corpse bit deep without Josh's instructions. He turned his head to the side, tearing skin and muscle.

"Enough!" Balthazar snarled. He grabbed Hicks by the back of the neck and pulled him off Langstrom, who dropped to the ground, his head hanging by slick, gleaming tendons and strands of muscle. Langstrom writhed on the ground, hissing and wailing, the thick, dark blood mixing with the dirt to make a gruesome mud.

Balthazar popped Hicks's head from his shoulders and let the body drop beside Langstrom's. Maxwell, Glory, Beatrice, and Donegan cried out simultaneously at the sight of the vampire holding Hicks's head in one outstretched palm, Hicks's teeth snapping and biting air. Balthazar sneered in distaste, then drove the index finger of his free hand into the middle of Hicks's forehead.

Josh felt his connection to Hicks break and the slick, wet heat left his body in a rush. He let out a grateful breath and, still on his knees, fell forward to curl into a ball on the ground. A moment later, he straightened up, rising to his knees, and fixed a steely gaze on Balthazar's face. The vampire stared at him a moment before letting Hicks's head roll out of his hand and thump into the dirt.

"You seem to have forgotten," Balthazar said, "I still have someone you care about."

And he was gone.

A tense silence filled the smithy. It stretched out for a long moment until Maxwell turned to Josh and said, "What kind of fucking witchcraft was that?"

THIRTEEN

Dex lay sweating and restless in the middle of a dream filled with feverish images of burning red eyes and sharp-edged shadows in candlelight. Interspersed among these visions, Dex saw flashes of Josh's face, his brow furrowed in concentration, eyes focused on a spot beyond Dex's sightline. A man stepped into view, tall and handsome in an Army uniform. This stranger's dark-eyed gaze was locked on Josh's face, and the intensity of his stare made jealousy flare within Dex's chest. A steaming rage coursed through him. There was something between Josh and this new arrival, something Dex didn't like, and even though Dex stood right beside Josh, it was as if Josh didn't see him. Even when Dex opened his mouth to scream at Josh, beg him for help, Josh kept his attention on the tall man in the Army uniform.

The high-pitched screams of the woman deeper inside the cave woke Dex, brought him shivering and gasping out of his dream. His neck ached where Balthazar had bitten him, and a dizzying nausea rolled through him like a dark, humid breeze when he sat up. Dex moaned and put his head in his hands, the chains on his wrists clanking quietly in the darkness.

He thought about the dream, felt the remnants of jealous rage slowly seeping out of him. It had felt as if he had been right there with Josh, watching him talk with the Army man. But Josh had ignored him, almost turned away from him, and Dex wondered just how real that interaction had been. He recalled the previous feelings he'd had about Josh, the comfort and relief he'd felt. He wished he could get that back again. In an effort to calm himself, he closed his eyes and thought about Josh, pictured his face, his smile, and the sound of his voice.

A change in the air around him shattered Dex's concentration. He sucked in his breath and lifted his head to squint toward the opening to the cave's chamber. He felt someone standing there, even though he couldn't see anyone for the darkness.

"Who's there?"

Something was different. It took a moment for Dex to realize the woman he thought could be Maureen Stanton had stopped screaming. In its absence, the silence felt oppressive, like a living thing that took up too much space. He let out his breath. Before he could pull in another, a strong hand grabbed him by the throat and easily lifted him off the floor. Dex kicked in the air and reached up to pry at the cold fingers gripping him, but it was like trying to dig through stone. It was, of course, Balthazar. The cold of his body seemed to crawl from his fingers and burrow into Dex's skin.

"You've been keeping secrets from me," Balthazar whispered. "Deeper secrets than I had first imagined."

"Don't know what…," Dex started, but he couldn't draw in enough breath to finish. His lungs burned, demanding air, and his throat ached.

"Your cowboy back in town is more powerful than I suspected," Balthazar said. "I knew he was special. I could smell it in his blood, but I did not realize what gift he possessed. You never mentioned his ability to raise the dead."

"Can't breathe," Dex choked out.

Balthazar made a small sound of disgust before releasing his grip. "You humans and your need for air and sunlight. You are such slaves to your bodies."

Dex fell to his knees, coughing and gasping as he gulped in air. Tears streamed from his eyes, and he angrily wiped them from his cheeks as he glared into the darkness where he thought Balthazar still stood. "You have no room to speak of us with such contempt. You crave the darkness and feed on blood. Who are you to cast judgment with your damned soul?"

A match burst into life across the chamber, forcing Dex to squint and turn in surprise to see Balthazar lighting the candle near the entrance. The flame took, jittering in a bit of draft and throwing the vampire's face into heavy shadow.

"You have steel inside you," Balthazar murmured in a low, sensual voice. "I do admire that. And your devotion to Josh Stanton is admirable, if outside the acceptance of those you live among." Balthazar approached him again, and Dex shrank back, averting his eyes. "Your blood is rich, Dexter Wells. Hearty. I could make a meal of you, and I just might. Would you enjoy it if I stripped the skin from you? Peeled it away and swallowed it here before you?"

Dex had no spit in his mouth, and his voice cracked as he

said, "No matter what you do to me, I will never become like you."

"No?" Balthazar leaned a little closer. "You can't begin to imagine the strength that flows inside me. The power I wield. All the creatures of the night are at my command. All your delicate townspeople are so afraid of what I might do to them on any whim. Isn't that what you've always dreamed of deep down in the blackest, most secret parts of yourself? Isn't that why you became a lawman, Dex? To feel that power?"

Dex shook his head. "No. You don't know anything about me."

"I've tasted your blood, Dex. I know more about you than you realize." Balthazar pressed his cold lips to Dex's ear and whispered, "Just two more bites, Dex. And you could live forever."

"As a blood drinking demon," Dex snarled. He made the mistake of pulling away from Balthazar and glaring into his glowing eyes. He was trapped at once, held by the red depths of that gaze. A cool calm rushed through him, relaxed his muscles and allowed his shoulders to lower. He could not look away from Balthazar's face, the prominent nose, red eyes, and thin slash of lips that hid his fangs.

"You kept something from me, Dexter," Balthazar whispered. "Something very important. Something I think you knew I would be very interested to learn."

He leaned closer, and Dex found he still had enough control to move back. It was a struggle, but he fought against the hold Balthazar had on him. He tried to imagine Josh there, felt a slight surge of power in his resistance, and managed to move even farther from Balthazar.

"Your resistance is still so strong," Balthazar said. "There's a will that burns within you. Imagine that will set free to do what it pleases, to treat others the way they deserve to be treated."

"I respect justice and the law," Dex said, but he knew Balthazar heard the quiver in his voice.

"Your man has a new attraction now, Dex," Balthazar said. "Your true love is drawn to another. To an Army man. To a man who wields more power than you with your simply shiny star."

Anger flared in Dex's chest, hot and fast, like a wildfire in a drought-starved forest. He felt it flash in his eyes, saw Balthazar's lip curl up in a cruel smile.

"Oh, you don't like that, do you? Oh my, no. You feel very possessive of Josh. But this new arrival, this sergeant, is stealing his attention. This Army man is helping him forget you, Dex, little by little."

Dex's anger fueled his resistance, and he was able to turn away from Balthazar, break their eye contact as he shook his head. The dream had been true. Someone new had arrived to steal Josh's affections. He clenched his jaw and shut his eyes, pushed back against the dark thoughts slinking inside his head. No, that was not Josh. He had to keep that foremost in his mind. Josh loved him and would never hurt him.

He risked a look back at Balthazar. "No. That's a lie. Josh will not forsake me."

"Maybe not yet, but rest assured he is tempted," Balthazar said. "Let me ease your mind, Dex. Let me make you feel better. I can help you, if you let me."

He was trapped inside the red of Balthazar's gaze once again. The struggle against the vampire was wearing him down, like a fever run amuck. Dex could no longer resist the vampire's hold, and he wasn't sure he wanted to. Perhaps he needed to change to get Josh back from this new man. Maybe if he had the same power as Balthazar, he could harness it, rein it in, and use it to keep Josh and the entire town safe.

Though a voice from deep inside screamed for Dex to move, to look away and break Balthazar's hold on him, it was quiet and weak now. Dex felt his will crumble away and he knelt before Balthazar, very still and calm. Balthazar's breath was as cold as his touch and smelled of death, but Dex did not blink or flinch. All he saw, all that mattered, was Balthazar's red glowing eyes.

"I think you are going to enjoy this, Dex," Balthazar said. "Josh has a new attraction, it's only right you should have one, too. It's been many years since I've satisfied my sexual appetites. Perhaps you'd like to see what kind of sexual skills a man can learn with centuries of time at his disposal? Would that interest you, Dexter?"

"Yes." Dex started to stretch out on the stone floor.

"Oh, no, that will never do," Balthazar said, producing a key from his shirt pocket. He unlocked Dex's bindings and picked him up with no effort at all. Dex felt cool wind on his skin, then Balthazar laid him back on the soft feather mattress in his private chamber.

Balthazar lit a candle and turned to Dex with a smile. He lightly touched Dex's chest, the cold skin of his finger spiking a chill through his body. Dex's cock bucked inside his breeches as the cold fingertip slid down his belly.

"You have always desired men?" Balthazar asked. His voice felt warm and smooth inside Dex's head, relaxing and calm, so unlike his touches.

Images flipped through Dex's mind as he thought of the men he had been attracted to over the years. The farm hands his father had hired; the son of a neighboring farmer who had helped during harvest; the town's previous deputy when Dex had been growing up, a man with broad shoulders and a cocky, sideways grin. And then he thought of Josh, remembered the first day they had met in the one room schoolhouse after Josh had been adopted by Agnes. He thought of the time they had spent together growing up, the friendship that had grown between them, and how that friendship had matured into love.

"Look at the size of you," Balthazar whispered after opening the buttons of Dex's breeches. "A fortunate find for me."

Balthazar put his lips around Dex's cock, and the chill embrace of the vampire's mouth sent a shudder through him. Dex felt the scratch of Balthazar's fangs and shivered as he imagined them biting into that most sensitive flesh. Then he felt the cold touch of Balthazar's fingers on his balls and he moaned. The coolness on his heated skin felt good, more erotic than Dex would have imagined, and he groaned as Balthazar sucked him.

Memories of Josh collided with thoughts of what Balthazar was doing to him, and Dex turned his head back and forth on the comfortable mattress. He could picture Josh above him, see the cross he had given to him for protection their final night together swinging between them, the expression on Josh's face relaxed and softened by love. Could Josh really stay true to their love? Dex had been missing for some time now, but was it long enough for Josh to seek out someone new?

Balthazar distracted Dex from thoughts of Josh by doing amazing things with his tongue, mouth, and fingers, and Dex lost all train of thought as he writhed beneath his touch. A cold finger slowly circled his tightened asshole before dipping in then out and continuing to circle, all the while Balthazar sucked his cock.

As Dex rose closer to climax, he lifted his hands overhead to grab fistfuls of the linen sheets, damp from the cool cave air.

"Close," he whispered.

Balthazar moved faster, much faster, his mouth a cool, quick stroke along the hardened post of Dex's cock. No man could ever move his head that quickly, and the speed of it brought Dex to a gasping, shouting finish. Balthazar did not lift his head, gulping down his seed before he let Dex's cock fall from between his lips.

"I have satisfied you," Balthazar said, his voice soft and edged with frost. "And now I would like to be compensated."

Balthazar used one hand to effortlessly lift Dex to sit on the edge of the mattress, then, with a rustle of fabric, dropped his breeches to expose thighs pale as cream, covered with dark hair. The tail of his shirt hung low, keeping his crotch from view until, with deft flicks of his fingers, Balthazar released the buttons and slid the shirt off. His chest was broad and muscular, sporting scars from swords and the long, rumpled mark of an old burn on the left side of his torso partially hidden by a thick layer of dark hair. Dex ran his fingers over the skin scarred by fire, his touch light.

"Someone burned you," Dex said. "Before—?"

"I turned vampire?" Balthazar finished for him. Then his voice, usually so strong and commanding, softened and became heavy with memory. "Yes. It is an old wound, far older than I care to remember. The betrayal that lays at the heart of its telling still pains me hundreds of years later."

"A lover?" Dex wondered.

"A brother," Balthazar said. "In blood as well as in eternity."

"You and your brother are both vampires?" Dex asked. He had never considered a family of vampires, and the thought sent a chill through him.

"We are. Both of us turned by a great and powerful vampire from my home country." Balthazar sighed. "In life, my brother was erratic, prone to bursts of anger and violent acts. He burned our home to the ground with our mother and father locked inside." Balthazar ran his fingers along the burn in his skin. "I was lucky and made it out. It took me many months to heal and many more to find my brother. Before I could exact my revenge, we were set upon and taken to our master's lair."

Dex was amazed at the thought of all this human drama entwined with an immortal creature of the night. "You've seen so much."

"More than you can imagine, Dexter Wells," Balthazar said. "Much more. When I was banished here to your poisonous valley by my brother, I had no hope of ever getting back to my home country. I expected to waste away in this cave as I fed on wolves, the occasional unfortunate traveler, and the members of the Indian tribe. But then your town was built, and the mine opened, and I found, shall we say, heartier food for the taking. And now I've established a loyal following of my own. Maybe some day, I can take the fight back to Lyonis and banish him." Balthazar stopped and smiled down at Dex, the vampire's fangs dimpling his lower lip. He stroked a cold finger down Dex's cheek and cupped his chin in his hand. "But that was a long time ago, and is of no matter to us at this moment."

A thought drifted up from the black lake of lust that had

flooded Dex's mind, and he dropped his gaze to the creases of scar tissue along Balthazar's side. The thought was of how he loved Josh and how Balthazar was tricking him into sex. Dex knew that he should try to run; he should turn away and flee down the cave passage until he reached the entrance. He needed to get away from here, away from Balthazar, and back to Josh, back to Belkin's Pass where he was loved and needed.

"Dex."

The sound of his name drew his attention, and he fell once more into the depths of Balthazar's red-eyed gaze. Thoughts of escape sunk beneath the surface of that black lake inside his mind, and Dex focused on the darkened circles of Balthazar's hardened nipples. He pinched them, felt the cold hard points beneath his fingers like frozen nail heads. He ran his gaze down Balthazar's flat, hairy belly, darting left to right to follow the line of battle scars lower and lower to the thick shaft that pointed accusingly at Dex from its nest of wiry black hair. As Dex stared at the hooded cock, a drop of thick clear fluid gathered at the tip and fell in a long runner onto Dex's thigh where its cold touch made him shiver.

"Quid pro quo," Balthazar said.

Dex looked up, trapped anew by the red-eyed stare that drowned any resistance. "I don't know what that means."

"It means I did something for you," Balthazar explained. "Now you do something for me."

With a quick nod, Dex leaned in. He closed his eyes as he opened his mouth. He smelled dirt and something slightly floral before the hard, cold length of Balthazar's cock slid between his lips. The skin tasted of dirt mixed with a tang of spice. It was cold where it lay along his tongue, and his teeth ached from it.

And, yet, Dex could not pull away. He felt himself grow hard again as he sucked, slowly at first but quickly picking up speed. His lips grew numb from touching Balthazar's skin, yet his cock throbbed with renewed need at the feel of a man in his mouth. All thoughts of his life before left him, all thoughts of Josh, and the only thing that mattered was pleasing Balthazar.

"Faster," the vampire commanded. "Yes, that's it. Like that. Just a little longer. Close." His voice deepened, and he called out in a language Dex did not understand, then his cock jerked inside Dex's mouth and thick, cold semen erupted. Dex swallowed it down, wincing as the cold reached out from his stomach and made his limbs shiver.

"You have promise, Dexter Wells," Balthazar said, and pulled his hips back to let his cock slip free of Dex's lips. "You would make a worthy partner." He leaned down to place his lips beside Dex's ear. "And now, I must feed. Your lover kept me from that tonight with his tricks, and so you pay his price."

Bright pain seared into his neck and Dex closed his eyes as he opened his mouth, hearing his scream echoed back to him from the woman across the chamber.

CHAPTER

FOURTEEN

A loud clanging brought Glory awake with a start. She sat up in the pile of hay where she had practically fallen over asleep several hours ago. Her mind was muddled, and the scene before her made her feel even more confused. Donegan stood by the forge, the muscles of his bare chest standing out as sweat ran down his torso. He leaned closer to the flames of the forge, using metal tongs to remove the stone crucible. His gaze was sharp, focused on the task at hand even though heavy shadows darkened the skin under his eyes. The man had to be exhausted as he'd been awake for more than a day.

Josh stood nearby, his gaze just as sharply focused as he watched Donegan pour steaming silver liquid into molds. Though the blacksmith had been awake all night, Donegan's hands did not shake, and the liquid metal flowed smoothly. There had been much discussion about the types of weapons that should be forged, until finally it was decided a number of short swords and knives, sharp-ended pikes, and round musket balls would be best.

A heavy snore from beside Glory startled her, and she jumped away. When she looked back, a nervous laugh slipped out at the sight of Beatrice sprawled on her back in the hay, mouth hanging open and a great amount of cleavage showing beneath the chemise because the man's shirt she wore had come unbuttoned. Glory blew out a breath and crawled back across the hay. Her movement attracted the attention of Donegan as the blacksmith finished pouring the silver, and his gaze locked onto Beatrice's chest.

"Smithy Donegan," Glory said in a sharp tone as she pulled Beatrice's shirt back together. "Avert your eyes. She may be a whore, but she still deserves respect."

To his credit, Donegan blushed and looked away. Glory saw Josh flick his gaze toward Beatrice, smile briefly, then turn away. Sergeant Walker Maxwell sat by the locked doors, a rifle across his knees, his narrowed eyes shifting to follow Josh's movements around the room. The sergeant had removed Josh's bindings after Balthazar had left them, but he kept his gaze on him as if afraid Josh might escape the minute he left his sight.

The other townspeople had taken up spots in the corners, talking quietly among themselves and casting nervous glances at the rest of them. After witnessing Josh's ability to raise the dead the night before, the group was naturally leery of them all.

Beatrice snorted and shifted in her sleep, the shirt buttons popping open again. Glory sighed and reached out to tug the shirt closed once more. This time, Glory's touch startled Beatrice awake, and she shoved Glory back with a hand to her chest. The warmth of Ohanzee's spirit flashed around her as Beatrice sat up, her eyes wild but unfocused with sleep, a small knife clutched in her fist.

Glory relaxed and let Ohanzee take over. He rolled her out of Beatrice's reach as she slashed. Glory could feel the pressure of his arms around her, the heat of his chin on her shoulder as he rolled her through the hay. They came to a stop several feet away, Ohanzee lying atop her, his dark-eyed gaze holding hers, the hard line of his cock pressing against her thigh, invisible to all but her. Glory smiled up at him, but even as she reached for Ohanzee, fingers straining to feel the touch of his skin, he began to fade. The danger had passed; Josh and Donegan had run over to disarm Beatrice and shake her fully awake, and Glory felt Ohanzee's presence melting away.

Before he left her completely, however, Ohanzee surprised her by leaning closer. Glory thought he meant to kiss her, a simple kiss goodbye, their first, and she closed her eyes. Instead of a kiss, however, Ohanzee's lips brushed against her ear, the touch so light it might have been a small breeze. But then she heard a word, whispered so quietly in his fading voice it might instead have been a stray thought in her head: "Crystals."

She opened her eyes to see only the smithy's ceiling above her. Ohanzee had gone again. The danger had passed, and she was on her own.

"Glory, I'm so sorry," Beatrice said in her loud, brassy voice. "I didn't know it was you, I swear on all I love."

Glory sat up and gave Beatrice what she hoped was a reassuring smile. "We're all jumpy, Bea. It's all right."

"Sun's up."

Glory looked over at Maxwell who had gotten to his feet by the door. He peered between boards at the window, a thin stripe of sunlight lying along one of his mutton chop sideburns.

"Praise God," Donegan said. Glory noticed the black-smith kept glancing at Beatrice and looking shyly away. Well, perhaps Donegan was more of a gentleman than she might have given him credit for, and it appeared as if he might have a bit of a spark for Beatrice.

Josh approached her, a concerned expression on his face. "You hurt?"

Glory shook her head. "No. He... I was able to get away."

Josh's brown eyes narrowed. "Your spirit saved you?"

Glory nodded. She and Josh had never actually discussed Ohanzee, but she knew he realized she had some kind of protection. And right now she needed to share with someone the different way Ohanzee had acted. "He spoke this time."

"He's never spoken before?"

Glory shook her head.

"What did he say?"

"Crystals."

Josh frowned. "Crystals? What does that mean?"

Glory shook her head. "Not sure. My people use crystals for many things." She took a breath, thought about the single word Ohanzee had whispered. "I just don't know what he tried to tell me. He has never spoken to me before."

"That surprises me. How long has he been with you?"

"My father cast the protective spell when I was very young. Six years old, if I recall."

Josh raised his eyebrows. "That young? Why did he think you needed such protection?"

Glory felt her jaw tighten. Before she could stop herself, she said, "To protect me from the mob of white men who came to take him from our home and hang him because he had married a white woman."

A blush colored Josh's cheeks and he looked away. "Oh."

"I'm sorry, Josh," Glory said, embarrassed for him and upset at herself for lashing out over something he had no hand in. He was an outcast as well, a witch, and a sodomite to boot. She had no right to treat him bad.

He looked her in the eye and smiled tightly. "Well, for the record, I'm sorry, too."

Glory gave a quick nod. "I know. We're all outcasts now, aren't we?"

Outcasts, just like she and her best friend Edith used to call themselves. She thought fleetingly of Edith, felt the pang of guilt over the fact that Balthazar had turned her. But at that time Glory did not realize what he was, or the danger they all were in. She wondered what special errand Balthazar had sent Edith on, and then she pushed the contemplation aside. There were things to do, and worrying about what was out of her control would do none of them any good. As her mother had told her when she was young, things outside of your reach are just that. She wasn't sure she believed that to be true in all cases, but it was good to be able to tell the difference.

The sergeant pulled the doors open wide and sunlight filled the smithy. They all took deep, grateful breaths of the cool breeze that blew in. Maxwell stepped outside with his rifle held in both hands, back straight, broad shoulders tight with tension. He looked up and down the street, then turned to face them.

"I need to get back to the fort," Maxwell said.

Glory noticed the sergeant staring at Josh, and Josh staring right back. The moment stretched out until, finally, Josh looked away from the sergeant with a blush coloring his cheeks. There was something between the two men, an attraction she had seen before in the saloon, usually between one of the girls and a man she fancied over the others. Glory kept her thoughts to herself, unsure if it was her place to say anything. She and Josh had been through a lot together, but they really didn't know each other very well. And she knew Josh's heart was with Dex. At least, she thought it was.

"We should search the town," Glory said, drawing the attention of both men. "Gather what weapons we can and other supplies before we ride out to find Dex. Search for other survivors."

Josh nodded and looked back at Maxwell. "Will you come back? We need the help, as you could see last night."

"You managed pretty well on your own." Maxwell glanced out at the remains of Private Hicks and his horse, scattered throughout the night by scavengers. "Never really heard what it is you can do."

"Don't really know myself," Josh said, dropping his gaze and blushing. "Just always happened to me."

Maxwell nodded. "Must have been hell growing up with that secret. I know a bit about that kind of thing." He looked toward Glory, noticed her listening, and turned away suddenly with a blush on his cheeks. A moment passed before he looked back over his shoulder, gaze fixed mostly on Josh. "I will come back, and with more men. Not sure how many will be on their feet by the time I get there."

A cold shiver stitched up Glory's spine, and she stepped forward to ask, "What do you mean?"

Maxwell fixed his gaze on her. "About three quarters of my troops have taken ill. I'm hoping they're off their bunks and up and about soon."

"Ill how?" Glory asked.

"Chills, wore out. Some kind of sickness being passed around."

Beatrice moved up to stand beside Glory and said, "Sounds an awful lot like how the girls at the One-Eyed Rooster were acting."

"Beatrice is right," Glory agreed. "Your men may have been bitten by a vampire like those you saw last night. They could be turning into vampires now, if they haven't already."

"Sweet mother of God," Donegan whispered. From the corner of her eye, Glory saw the man cross himself. The new group of townspeople had gathered behind the blacksmith to listen.

"Well, then, I should arm myself." Maxwell walked across the room to assess the weapons. He pulled on his gloves and plucked a thin silver sword from the meager stash.

"Hey!" one of the men behind Donegan said. He shrank back when Maxwell turned his cold glare on him, but Glory had to admire the man's bravery when he followed through with what he had to say. "You saw what happened last night. We're going to need every weapon we can get to keep the wolves and those demons at bay."

Maxwell walked right up to stand before the man, towering a good foot over him. "What's your name?"

"D-Dooley," the man said. "Arnold Dooley."

"Well, Arnold Dooley, I need to ride twenty miles on my own to Fort Emmerick where most of my men may already have been turned into these vampires." Maxwell tipped his head toward Donegan. "Since you have the blacksmith here to keep making you weapons, I'm pretty sure the one sword I'm taking for my own protection won't be missed. Do you agree?"

Dooley mumbled something, and Maxwell leaned closer to the man. "Sorry, Dooley, I couldn't hear you."

"I agree," Dooley said in a louder voice, stepping back behind Donegan once again.

"Glad to hear it," Maxwell said. He slipped the sword into his belt and when he looked up at them again, his expression was grim. "Guess I'm ready for them now."

"In the heart," Josh said.

"And cut off their heads," Beatrice added. "Afterward."

Maxwell stared at them for a moment, his face pale and eyes wide. Then, with a tight-lipped nod, he took his horse's reins and led it out into the street. After climbing into the saddle, he looked down at Josh once more. "I'll come back as soon as I can. And I'll bring as much firepower as I'm able." He nodded down to Hicks's remains. "I trust you'll treat Private Hicks with the respect he deserves."

Josh nodded up at him. "We'll see to it he gets a proper burial."

Beatrice held up a hand and hurried back into the smithy, returning a moment later with the sergeant's bindings. She held them up, sunlight sparking off the dull metal. "You forgot these."

Josh narrowed his eyes at the bindings then shot Maxwell a look that appeared to be half-anger and half-interest.

"Yes, Walker," Josh said, his use of the man's forename making Glory raise her eyebrows. "You don't want to leave your bindings behind."

Walker Maxwell turned his horse, looked back over his shoulder and said with a smirk, "You keep 'em for me until I get back." Then, he snapped the reins and his horse bolted down the street, eager, it seemed, to be away from Belkin's Pass.

Glory watched the sergeant ride off, then looked up and down the deserted street and decided she couldn't blame the man or his horse. She wished she had been able to go with them.

"Let's get started," Josh said to her. "We have a lot to do and need to leave by sunrise tomorrow. Dex has been gone for too long as it is."

FIFTEEN

Late in the afternoon, Josh stepped into a house a mile outside of town and paused to listen. No sounds from the other room or the sleeping loft above. Dust on the sideboard and fireplace mantle gave evidence the house had been abandoned for a while. He held a silver knife in one hand and a muzzleloader packed with a silver ball in the other as he advanced carefully. He only had four sharpened wooden stakes left in the pack slung over one shoulder, and maybe half a dozen silver musket balls in a pouch that hung off his belt.

It had been a busy afternoon of staking vampires.

Moving through both of the lower rooms, Josh stopped when he found a hinged door set into the floor in a corner of the cooking area. A root cellar, the perfect place for vampires to go to ground. He set aside the rifle and pack on the floor nearby, took a steadying breath, then pulled up the door.

The smell wrapped around him, heavy and nauseating. It was the smell of death and rot, and Josh put a hand over his nose and mouth, looking away as he blinked tears from his eyes.

Vampires, most definitely.

Standing, Josh grabbed a lantern off the mantle and used a match from a nearby box to light the candle inside. He withdrew two stakes from the pack, then paused to think. If he remembered correctly, this house belonged to Wyatt Abbott, his wife Elaine, and their two young children. With a wince, he pulled out his last two stakes. Before he could consider what waited for him below, he climbed down the short ladder into the root cellar.

The yellow candlelight flickered across the cellar. Shadows twitched and ducked along shelves layered with potatoes, salted meats, dried herbs, and canned goods. Josh's stomach rumbled at the sight of the meat, and he realized he had not yet taken a meal that day.

Thoughts of food were forgotten, however, when the lantern light revealed a pair of men's boots lying toes up on the floor of the cellar. Josh stepped closer and licked his suddenly dry lips as a shiver worked through him. Wyatt Abbott lay on the dirt floor of the cellar, pale hands crossed over his chest. His wife Elaine lay nearby, her face still and beautiful, hair loose and spread out behind her head.

Between them lay both children, a young boy of about eight and a girl no more than five. The boy wore overalls that looked too short for his legs, legs that would never grown another inch. The girl wore a dirt and bloodstained dress that had once been white and edged with lace, her hair a tangled blonde mess.

"Dear God," Josh whispered.

He knelt in the dirt beside them, set the lantern aside,

and took one of the stakes in his hands, repeatedly adjusting his fingers around its length as he looked over the grouping of the bodies. It would be easiest, and less messy, to start with Elaine who lay against the back wall, but Josh would have to lean over the rest of the family to do that. He had time, the sun would be up for hours yet, but to be in such close proximity to vampires was unnerving.

Josh unbuttoned his shirt, allowing Dex's cross to swing free. He gripped the stake tight, adjusted his position, and stretched out over Wyatt and the two children, deeper into the cellar shadows. Hovering above Elaine, he braced himself with one hand on the back wall. He raised the wooden stake, paused to take a steadying breath, and then stabbed it down hard into Elaine's chest.

The woman's eyes opened wide, angry red embers in the dark shadows of the cellar. She screamed, a long, loud scream that forced Josh back, covering his ears and screaming himself. A flood of thick, vile smelling black fluid bubbled out of her mouth. Her hands, twisted into claws, reached for him, slinging drops of the black stuff across his face. Josh turned away and clamped his lips tight to avoid getting any of it in his mouth. When he looked back, Elaine's body had sunken in on itself, the smooth marble skin of her face flaking away into dust.

Josh dragged his sleeve across his mouth as he watched her body fall apart. Before he could lose his nerve, he took up the stake in shaking hands, lifted it over Wyatt's chest, and brought it down hard. Wyatt grabbed him, fingers tight around Josh's wrist, grinding together bone and making Josh scream in pain. Thick black blood poured from his mouth and pooled around Josh's knees as he struggled to pull his wrist free of Wyatt's cold tight grip. Finally, the red light in Wyatt's eyes faded, and his skin turned gray and flaked away. When Josh pulled back again, Wyatt's fingers snapped off and spun around his wrist like a macabre bracelet.

"Jesus," Josh said through a gasp and pried the fingers off, tossing them into the shadows of the cellar as shudders wracked his body.

Now he had to stake the children.

"Lord, give me strength," Josh whispered.

He decided to leave the stake in Wyatt's crumbling chest —too spooked to risk pulling it free—and took up his second to last one. He moved up beside the flattened body of Wyatt, his knees mired in the thick, horrid mess of black blood. Looking between the boy and his sister, Josh's will faltered. He sat back on his heels and took a few deep breaths, head turned away from the stench of what he knelt in. When he was ready, he rose up, adjusted his fingers on the stake, and plunged it down into the boy's chest.

The crack of bone and feeling of resistance brought up his gorge and, as the boy shrieked and clawed at the wooden stake, Josh turned away to vomit. By the time he looked back, the boy had gone, his hands bony claws that still gripped the stake. As Josh knelt and stared, the boy's jaw fell off his skull with a thin, wet sound that Josh knew would stay with him forever.

Only the girl was left. Her dress, white before she'd been turned, was now splattered with dried blood from her feedings as well as splatters of black blood from her family being staked. Flakes of ash had caught on the damp material, shriveled skin from the rest of her family.

The boy's skeletal fingers still clung to the stake in his

chest, so Josh took up the final one he had and held it over her. He felt the thump of Dex's cross against his breastbone as he moved, heard the call of a bird from outside the cabin and the scuttle of rodents nearby. Josh took a breath, held it a moment, and then said, "Rest in peace," in a hoarse croak.

The stake crushed her breastbone like it was a skim of ice after a quick frost. Her tiny fingers closed on his wrist, the nails digging into his skin. The red cinders of her eyes glared up at him, and her narrow lips pulled back from tiny, wickedly pointed fangs. She snapped at his wrist, and Josh jerked his arm back just in time, feeling the motion yank her arm from its socket as her body withered. Her final breath gusted into his face, reeking of death, and Josh turned away again to cough up the little left in his belly.

Josh climbed out of the cellar and let the door fall shut. He blew out the candle before returning the lantern to its place on the mantle. Dust spun through the sunlight that lit lacy white curtains at the window, inviting Josh to rub the thin material between his fingers. His touch left smudges of black blood on the delicate curtains, and he tightened his lips and turned away. He took up his rifle, secured the silver knife, and grabbed his empty pack. He considered going back for the hunks of preserved meat in the cellar, but the thought of the four bodies waiting for him, all now turned to dust, kept him from returning, and he left the cabin.

Josh slid his rifle into the straps of the saddle on Clementine's back, secured the empty pack, then crossed to the water pump. It hadn't been used in quite a while and he gritted his teeth as he worked the handle. Sweat ran down his face and back, and the muscles of his shoulders ached with the effort. Just when he was about to give up, the pump gurgled and a flood of clear, cold water rushed out to spatter on the ground.

Josh splashed water on his face, ducked his head beneath and let the biting cold water snap his senses back to life. He took up a bucket lying nearby, filled it, and carried it to Clementine. As the horse drank, Josh patted her neck and inspected the healing wolf bites and scratches on her legs, trying to push the memory of the Abbott girl from his mind.

On his ride back into town, Josh turned occasionally to look over his shoulder. The road behind him stretched off across the flatlands toward the distant mountain range and the desert land known locally as Venom Valley. It was where Balthazar held Dex. Josh knew the vampire had ulterior motives for keeping Dex, most likely as bait to lure Josh himself into his territory to overpower him. He would most likely turn Josh into a vampire who would then be under Balthazar's command, then the vampire could use Josh's power to raise the dead.

Thinking about Dex set off conflicting emotions. His chest tightened and a blush heated his face, despite the cold water he had doused himself with. A blend of attraction and a nervous urgency to rescue Dex from Balthazar's hold seemed to swirl within him, like a dust devil out in Venom Valley. He knew Sergeant Maxwell and Glory were right; they needed to find more weapons and organize before they could ride off into Venom Valley. But the helpless feeling of time slipping past, each second another chance for Balthazar to kill Dex or, worse, turn him into a bloodthirsty vampire, made Josh impatient and edgy. They needed help, and the Army would be more than enough.

The thought of Sergeant Maxwell kicked his pulse up as well, but Josh told himself it was because the man angered him, and not because Josh was attracted to him. Josh loved Dex, that was all there was to it. Even though Sergeant Maxwell was handsome and strong and brave, Josh knew Dex was all those things and more. And he had years of friendship with Dex.

Clementine knew the road, and, as she clopped along, Josh took a few moments to close his eyes. He thought back on his years spent getting to know Dex, smiling as his cock hardened. Josh was eager to have Dex home, here in Belkin's Pass and standing beside him. He wanted to strategize with Dex, looked forward to touching the man again, kissing him, tasting him.

Josh imagined seeing Dex again. The touch of Dex's lips would send a wave of need through Josh. He would feel the press of Dex's hard length against his own, feel the heavy, sweat-damp touch as Dex reached down the front of his breeches to clutch Josh tight, all the while kissing him, tongues rolling together.

He imagined welcoming Dex home, fantasized about staying up all night with him. As he imagined the things he would do to welcome Dex, Josh stretched out his feelings, opened his mind to Dex in an effort to make that connection with him once again. But there was no response, and Josh's hope floundered. Had he taken too long to organize an attack on Balthazar? Had the vampire killed Dex? Or turned him perhaps? Made him into a vicious, blood-hungry night walker?

Josh refused to believe that. He couldn't allow himself to

lose hope. Dex was alive, he had to be. With a breath, Josh returned his thoughts to welcoming Dex, imagined the man's body, the hair on his chest, the thick dark patch of hair at the base of his sturdy cock. He recalled how it had felt to hold Dex's prick in his hand, to feel its hardened heat as he stroked it, tasted it, felt it push deep inside him.

A flicker of a connection wavered within Josh's chest, and he sucked in a quick breath.

Dex. He was alive, Josh had felt it. Alive but... weak, hurt. Where once Josh had felt openness and a desperate welcome, now he felt wariness and doubt. What had happened to Dex to change him? Even in the quick glimpse Josh had been able to catch, he had sensed something dark within Dex, something leery and suspect.

"Dex," Josh whispered. "No, don't let him get to you."

Josh tried to conjure up the connection again. He thought about Dex's hands on him, Dex's cock inside him, and went through the most intimate of their memories, but nothing worked. He received no sense that Dex was hearing him any longer.

Clementine snorted and tossed her head, and Josh opened his eyes. He looked around to find he was already at the edge of town. That made him feel relieved, but he was troubled by what he had felt during his connection with Dex. Was it too late for him to save Dex? Was Dex too far gone? Had Balthazar poisoned not just Dex's body, but his mind as well? Turned him against Josh?

An aching sadness churned within him as he considered this possibility. What if he was able to save Dex only to lose him? What if what Dex was going through changed him forever? Left Dex unable to be with him, unable to love him? Could Josh live through losing Dex?

"I gotta get him back," Josh said to himself, "one way or the other."

Thus decided, Josh kicked his heels to get Clementine to trot a little faster. Time was slipping past too fast, and now that he knew Dex suffered even more than he had imagined, the urgency to save him expanded. Too much time had been wasted on planning and gathering. They had to act.

SIXTEEN

The wrist cuff was tighter since Balthazar returned Dex to his alcove in the cave. But Dex was determined to escape. He still tasted dirt in his mouth from his night with Balthazar, and Dex didn't think he could withstand another encounter like that.

His cock hardened fast at the memory of being with Balthazar, and Dex determinedly turned away from the attraction that simmered low in his belly. He didn't want Balthazar; he wanted Josh. He *needed* Josh. And he needed to get back to Belkin's Pass to stop Josh from turning to the Army man for comfort. He had to show Josh who he belonged to.

Dex stopped in his struggle against the cuff and stared into the darkness before him. Where had that thought come from? He didn't own Josh. He loved Josh, and wanted Josh to be happy. Didn't he?

Of course he did. And that stray thought, that quick glint of wickedness, was all the more reason for him to escape. If he stayed here any longer, Balthazar would continue to work on twisting Dex's feelings around until he could no longer recognize himself.

He gripped the left cuff with his right hand, ignored the pain in his forearm from the deep bruising and slowly healing cut, and twisted it back and forth. The edge bit into the chafed, tender skin of his wrist, but he kept at it. Blood welled up from the wound, oozed beneath the cuff, and spilled to the cave floor between his feet.

A tingle shot up his arm from a particularly deep cut, and Dex swore into the choking darkness around him. Trying to pull his hand through the cuff was hard enough, but trying to do it in a pitch-black cave was close to impossible.

But he had to get out. He needed to get back home, back to Josh. If he stayed in this cave another night, Balthazar would turn him. Dex would rather take his chances in Venom Valley than spend eternity avoiding the sunlight and craving the taste of blood.

Dex cradled his arm, hugged his shackled wrist tight to his chest, and felt the hot, slick smear of blood across his skin. He moaned quietly as he rocked back and forth, working up the nerve and energy to try again. He was exhausted. His mind played tricks on him here in the dark, echoing cave, making him think he heard the scuff of Balthazar's shoe or felt the draft of his fast movements.

"Get hold of yourself," he whispered into the darkness. "You can do this."

He started twisting and pulling his left arm again, feeling the cuff dig into his already swollen and throbbing thumb. As he worked, sweat ran down his face and blood spattered on his boot. He shifted his foot, moving it out from under the blood, and he heard the quiet clink of metal as the toe of his boot struck something on the floor. It hadn't been the chain. He knew where that was. This was something different, something smaller.

A flash of memory lifted his hopes, and he stopped all movement as he thought back on the previous night. He remembered Balthazar unlocking the cuffs before carrying him to the larger cave chamber and laying him on the bed. With a wince, he skipped over what happened after that and thought about when Balthazar had brought him back in here to chain him up once again. Had Dex heard the quiet clink of the key falling from Balthazar's pocket? How had the vampire missed that sound with his heightened senses? Could this be an elaborate trap of some kind? But maybe Balthazar had not noticed he dropped the key because it had been close to sunrise, and he had been rushing to get to his coffin.

Dex dropped to his hands and knees, wincing at the pain that spiraled up his arm as he put weight on it. His thumb felt hot and pained at the touch from his previous escape attempt. He felt around on the dirt floor strewn with rocks, tossing the stones out of the way as the chain dragged behind him. Nothing. Perhaps the chain had hit the key and sent it tumbling off into the darkness.

Fatigue washed over him, filled him, and Dex became so weary he had to lie on his side. He pulled his knees to his chest and closed his eyes, promising the part of himself that protested he would only rest for a moment. He took long, slow breaths to steady himself, and when he felt ready, he reached out to gently pat the dirt around him. When that area had been searched, he forced himself to sit up, shift position, and repeat the process.

His frustration built, gnawing away his patience and

slow, easy movements. He had to move faster, had to escape, had to be free during daylight hours, no matter how tired he was, no matter how much pain he was in.

The key was here, he knew it. He could feel it.

More gentle patting followed by a shifting of position. The chain dragged across the dirt after him, pulling on the cuffs and sending bites of pain through his left arm.

After what felt like hours, he turned to lie in the opposite direction and reached out, his eyes closed and fingers jerking away in surprise at the cool metal touch of a small key. He gasped and sat up, then realized he'd lost the position of the key. Dex drew in a breath, held it, and lay back down in the approximate position he had been in before. He released his breath in a slow, steady stream and put out his hand. His fingers touched the edge of the key, and he pulled it into his palm and sat up. He held the key tight in his fist and pressed it against his chest as tears filled his eyes and spilled down his cheeks.

"Please God," he whispered into the darkness, "let it fit. Please just let it fit."

Dex held the key in his teeth and used the fingers of his right hand to feel around the cuff for the lock's keyhole. He touched the small hole and, keeping his thumb on it, lowered his head to carefully take the key from between his teeth. With one more quiet prayer, he slipped the key into the lock and twisted it. Sweat beaded across his forehead and dripped down his sides as his back muscles ached with tension. The key caught the tumblers, resisted a heart-stopping moment, and then turned. The lock released, and the cuff popped open.

He was almost free.

His left thumb was swollen and stubborn, and he

dropped the key twice. Each time he heard the high metal clink of its bounce, he knew in the cold dark corners of his heart that it would be gone for good. But each time a short, nerve-wracking search brought his fingers to it. Finally, he forced his swollen thumb to close hard on the key. He slipped it into the lock, twisted it, and the cuff on his right wrist opened and fell to the floor with a heavy clank.

A breathless, ragged laugh was all he could manage before he staggered to his feet and wavered for a moment. His shirt and pants were in tatters, but he was grateful he still had his boots. At the opening to what he considered his cell inside the cave, Dex paused as a wave of dizziness spun through him. He wondered if he hadn't lost more blood than anticipated from Balthazar's feedings as well as his injuries. He felt the blood dripping from the gouges around his left wrist, running over his hand and spilling on the stone floor.

He still clutched the key in his swollen, throbbing left hand and brought it to his lips for a gentle kiss before pocketing it. He didn't want to throw it away; it meant too much to him. He was going to hang onto that key for the rest of his life.

The woman deeper in the cave, the woman he was sure he had recognized, continued to scream as Dex stood at the opening to his own chamber. Forcing himself to take the first step, Dex lurched out into the cave passageway and turned right, away from the woman whose screams followed him. There was nothing he could do for her now, but he would tell Josh about his suspicions.

Thoughts of Josh urged Dex on and he kept the memory of him front and center in his mind. He thought about Josh's brown eyes, dark blond hair, and the smile that transformed Josh's usually serious face. Hope, having abandoned him since his imprisonment, now flickered to life inside him. Josh waited for him. Josh loved him. Josh had not forsaken him. That had been a mind trick played by Balthazar. Dex just needed to return to Josh to see the truth.

Encouraged and determined, Dex stepped around the rocks that littered the floor of the passage as he made his escape. It wasn't until he had moved to the other side of the cave to avoid a pile of stones and paused to catch his breath that Dex realized he could now see the obstacles in his path. A bit of light had worked its way back to him from the cave opening.

Not far now. He could do it. He would do it, for himself, and for Josh. Always for Josh.

Dex pushed off the side of the wall, cradled his hand against his chest, and stumbled toward freedom.

SEVENTEEN

A bullet punched through the back of the chair behind which Glory had taken refuge. It lodged into the wall behind her shoulder and she jumped, frightened despite the warm glow of Ohanzee around her. She felt the pressure of his hands gripping her upper arms, his chin resting on her shoulder, and his strong thighs on either side of her own.

Glory needed to see him again, needed to hopefully have him speak to her again. But to see him, she had to put herself in danger. And so she had come to the one place she knew she could find trouble.

"You half-breed whore bitch!" Sally's voice wobbled as much as she did, and she fired at the chair once again.

Ohanzee rolled Glory across the floor just in time to avoid the bullet that tore through the back of the chair. It hit the wall right where she'd been crouching. She came to a stop behind the other chair of the matched set and tried to make herself as small of a target as possible.

"Sally," Glory shouted. "You're ill. You need help. Come with me and we'll help you."

"I know what you're doing," Sally shrieked. "Don't think I don't. You want my money. That's all you've ever wanted from me. Well you're not going to get it. Balthazar will take care of me; he knows what I need."

"Oh?" Glory countered. "And has he brought you what you need?"

Another bullet was Sally's response, a wide shot that came nowhere close to Glory's hiding spot.

Glory turned her head to see Ohanzee, but all she could manage was a glimpse of the tip of his nose. Still, she felt his warmth around her, his body against her own, and the touch of his hands on her arms. If only she could focus on him long enough to talk with him. But the only time she saw him was when she was in danger, and she needed to keep her attention on the situation, especially when dealing with Sally. As much as Ohanzee was able to guide her movements during times of trouble, he could not seem to predict what Sally would do next. Glory suspected it was the absinthe Sally had drunk over the years that kept her thoughts clouded from him.

So, while she had definitely come to the right place to find trouble, it might prove to be more dangerous than she had realized. Sally was obviously suffering from her lack of absinthe and had become even more unpredictable. This might not have been such a good idea.

"Dammit," Sally muttered from across the room.

The sound of the woman working her old revolver came to Glory, and she felt Ohanzee squeeze her arms. It was now or never.

Glory was already running when she rose from behind the chair. But Sally had expected this, may have even set her up for it. Either way, Glory felt the hot nip of the bullet as it grazed her upper arm. She heard Ohanzee whisper something in Apache, then she had her hands on Sally and brought the woman to the floor beneath her.

Sally was thin and weak, and it took little time for Glory to disarm her as she sat on top of Sally and pinned her to the floor.

"Get off me! Leave me be!" Sally screamed, beating her tiny fists on Glory's chest.

Glory grabbed Sally's thin wrists in one hand and held them to the floor over the woman's head as she looked down into Sally's wide, crazed eyes.

"Sally, you're a danger to yourself and to the rest of us. You need to be cared for or you'll die."

"What do you care?" Sally said with a snarl. "You've always hated me."

"True," Glory replied, "but I don't trust you even more. I'd rather have you where I can keep an eye on you."

"Leave me alone, just leave me alone," Sally wailed as she turned her head away to cry.

Glory let Sally cry for a moment then, feeling the fight had gone out of her, released her hold and stood up. Glory turned her head to try and see Ohanzee as she felt his protective presence around her fading now that the immediate danger had passed, but he remained out of sight. Instead, Glory felt the touch of his lips against her ear, and she held her breath and listened closely to see if he would speak again.

"Crystals," Ohanzee whispered, and added, "Josh." Before Glory could shiver at the deep, smooth sound of his voice, he was gone.

Sally moaned from the floor. She had squeezed her eyes

shut and now rolled back and forth, hugging herself tight as if trying to keep from coming apart. "You bitch."

Glory turned away from Sally to look out the window at the wide expanse of prairie visible over the roof of the combination undertaker and carpenter shop across the street. She stared at the land and considered Ohanzee's words. "Crystals, Josh" led her to think about the crystals she had been given at the Indian camp which she kept secured in a deerskin pouch tucked inside her clothes.

"Wicked!" Sally shrieked from her place on the floor, glaring up at Glory.

"Hold your tongue, Sally," Glory snapped. She stepped to the window, looked at the velvet drapes a moment, and then tore down one side.

Sally cried out and raised her thin arms toward Glory. "Don't tear apart my beautiful room! It's all I have left. Just leave me here in peace and go."

Glory spread the drape on the floor beside Sally and, crouching by the woman's head, looked down into her frantic gaze. "You will never know peace, Sally."

"Leave go of her!"

Glory shot upright, fists clenched, Ohanzee's presence a sudden, muted heat around her as she stared at the broad figure that filled the shadowed doorframe. "Who is that?"

Beatrice stepped into the dusty sunlight, a wooden stake in each hand. When she saw it was Glory standing over Sally, she relaxed and lowered the stakes.

"Oh, it's you." Beatrice smiled at her. "I thought Sally was giving some poor woman from town a good shrieking, but I see it's just you settling your score."

"Good to see you, Bea," Glory said and gestured to the drape on the floor. "Give me a hand, yeah?"

A short time later, Glory and Beatrice carried Sally down the steps of the One-Eyed Rooster inside the tightly wound drapery. The woman wriggled and kicked as she shouted. They made their way through the ruins of the saloon and out the door onto the boardwalk. As they stepped down into the street, a man hailed them from the middle of town.

Glory stopped and turned to squint into the sun that sat just past noon. The man waved and walked slowly toward them, dressed in a white shirt and black pants held up with black suspenders.

"Who's that?" Beatrice whispered. Sally gave a wild kick, and Beatrice pinched her through the drape, smirking at Sally's shrieks. "Keep still!" Beatrice said.

"It's Doc Brandt," Glory said, and a cool, quiet breath of relief eased through her chest. "Doc Brandt's still alive. He can help us in case we get sick."

"You think he might be one a them?" Beatrice asked, eyes narrowed under her hat.

Glory shook her head. "He's out in the sunlight. If he was one of them, he'd burn up."

Beatrice nodded. "Yeah. That's right."

Doc Brandt approached and paused to catch his breath before he was able to talk. "Ladies, where have you been keeping yourselves?"

"We might ask the same of you," Beatrice snapped.

Doc Brandt looked startled at her tone, and his gaze jumped from Glory to Beatrice and back again. "Why, I've been off to Hainesville, taking care of Wanda Wainscott." He looked around at the empty street, shattered windows, and broken in doors. "What in the name of God happened here? Where is everyone? I've stopped in at home, and my wife and daughter are missing. Is it vandals?"

"Come with us, Doc," Glory said and tipped her head toward the blacksmith shop. "This is where what's left of us are spending our nights."

"The blacksmith's?" Doc asked as they started walking again. "Whatever for?"

"To stay safe from the vampires," Beatrice said.

"Vampires?" Doc stopped in his tracks, eyes wide and staring as Glory looked at him over her shoulder. "Have you all gone mad?" Sally kicked inside the drapery and shouted obscenities, attracting Doc's attention. "Who do you have wrapped up in there?"

"Sally," Beatrice said with a smug smile. "We don't trust her."

Doc stomped off down the street toward the sheriff's office. "Well, we'll just see what Sheriff Haden has to say about all this tomfoolery."

"Sheriff's dead," Glory called after him, and the man stopped in his tracks. He looked at her, his face pale. Sweat stood out on his forehead though a cool breeze kicked up dust devils around them. "Vampires got him and deputy Underwood." She turned to continue toward the blacksmith shop.

"W-what about Dexter Wells?" Doc asked, and from the sound of his voice Glory could tell he was following them.

"Gone," Glory replied as she entered the blacksmith shop. "Taken prisoner by a vampire. But Josh has a plan to get him back."

"Josh?" Doc Brandt hurried into the building after them. "Joshua Stanton? Is he here? He's wanted for murder, you know. He's an outlaw with a bounty on his head, and he could be dangerous. Where is he?"

"I'm here, doc," Josh said, stepping out of the shadows on the other side of the smithy. His shirt was off, and his suspenders dangled beside his legs. Sunlight reflected back from the gold cross that hung just beneath the hollow of his throat and shimmered in drops of water on his skin, left over from where he had been cleaning up at the washbasin in the corner. Dark blond hair covered his chest and belly, the skin beneath marred by a number of scabbed over scrapes and scratches.

Josh nodded to Glory and Beatrice, and then frowned at the tightly rolled drapery they still carried. "What have you brought us?"

"Someone I figured we should keep an eye on," Glory said. She dropped her end to the ground, Sally letting out a grunt just before Beatrice let her end fall as well. Glory pushed the lump with her foot and unrolled Sally from the drapery. They all stood around the tiny, disheveled woman as she gasped and coughed and tried to catch her breath.

"You evil bitch," Sally said to Glory. "This is kidnapping. I'll see you hung like your father."

Glory took a step toward Sally and drew back her foot to deliver a kick.

"Here now!" Doc Brandt shouted and clapped his hands. "That's enough!"

Glory glared at Sally before extending her arm toward Doc Brandt. "She shot me."

"What?" Josh and Doc Brandt both stepped closer.

"In self-defense! She attacked me!" Sally shouted, pointing at Glory. She looked around and crawled toward the doctor, the only possible ally of their small group. "She came into my rooms at the Rooster and tried to rob me!" She clutched at Brandt's legs, and his mouth turned down in distaste. "Said it was for all the years of low pay. But I pay my girls a damn sight better than any other saloon round here."

"Now, now, Sally," Doc Brandt said, taking a few steps back to escape her touch. "Let's not have accusations. Seems to me you'd want to stay with a group if the town is being overrun by wolves and... well, bandits."

"Worse than bandits," Josh said, his voice calm and edged with ice. "Murdering vampires is what they are. Led by one named Balthazar. He took Dex Wells, and we're fixin' to ride out tomorrow and bring him back."

Sally grew quiet and listened to Josh, her hair a wild halo around her head. Glory watched her expression, could almost hear the woman thinking about how to use Josh's plan to her advantage. Without a word, Glory stepped up and grabbed Sally by the arm, lifting her to her feet.

"Leave me go!" Sally shrieked. "Doc! Help! She means to kill me, help!"

"Shut your lying mouth," Glory said in a low voice as she led Sally into the shadows of the smithy. Somewhere in the back corner, she could hear the quiet snores of Donegan getting some rest after working all night forging silver into bullets and blades. The rest of the town survivors were nowhere to be found. After the demonstration of Josh's power over the dead the night before, she wouldn't be surprised if they didn't come back at all.

"I'm making sure you don't go trying to sell us out to Balthazar," Glory said as she pushed Sally into a small pile of hay. "But I'm not going to kill you." Glory moved quick, securing Sally's wrists with the bindings Sergeant Maxwell had left behind. She then attached the chain stretched between the bindings to a longer chain secured to the back wall of the smithy. "There. All the comforts of home."

"You can't keep me here!" Sally shouted at Glory's back as she returned to where Josh stood talking to Doc Brandt. "Release me this minute, do you hear me?"

Doc Brandt looked at the three of them in turn. "Are you saying my wife and daughter are dead?"

Josh cleared his throat and looked down at the dirt floor. "Most likely, Doc. I'm very sorry."

Doc Brandt's eyes grew glassy with tears, and he looked away out the door of the blacksmith shop. "I was only gone for three days. I don't think I even got to say goodbye to my daughter." He looked back at Josh. "You're sure of this?"

Glory spoke up before Josh could respond. "We don't know for sure, Doc. But we've been finding most of the town is either dead or turned. I'm very sorry." She moved her arm and winced at the pull of skin from where Sally's bullet had grazed her.

Doc Brandt cleared his throat, wiped his eyes, and stepped up to Glory as he extended his hand. "Let me have a look at that arm. It'll need to be cleaned up."

"Thanks, doc," Glory said.

"I wouldn't be much of a doctor if I didn't treat the people who needed me, now would I?" Doc Brandt mumbled.

Glory looked at Josh and said, "We should speak soon. I may be able to help you."

Josh frowned. "Help me? With what?"

Before Glory could reply, Beatrice cocked her head then

stepped to the doorway and peered down the street. "Someone's coming."

"Who is it?" Josh asked, approaching the door as well.

"Group of men on horses," Beatrice said. She turned to look at Glory, her eyes wide. "They're Injuns, Glory!"

CHAPTER

EIGHTEEN

Josh squinted against the sun as he looked down the street. Beatrice was right; the new arrivals were Indians, three of them. They rode single file and wore plains hats, jackets, and breeches made of deerskin. Their dark hair hung in long braids down their backs. One of the men wore an eye patch, and Josh remembered seeing him in the Indian camp above Venom Valley the day he and Glory had left to try and save Dex.

Josh went through the smithy to grab his shirt off the hook by the washstand. As he walked back to the open doors, he pushed his arms through the sleeves and buttoned it up, hearing Donegan snoring from one side of him as Sally shouted obscenities at him from the other.

"She going to lose her voice soon?" he asked Glory and Beatrice as he stepped up between them.

"Ain't happened for five years," Beatrice replied. "Cain't say it will now."

The Indians came to a stop and the man in the lead nodded before sliding off his horse. He dismounted and gestured for them to follow as he walked to the horse and rider bringing up the rear. Josh realized that the rider pulled behind him a travois made from sturdy branches and deer hide. A very still figure lay on the travois, bound to the branches by ropes and covered with blankets.

A tight, hot feeling clenched in the base of Josh's throat like a fist, blocking his breath. He didn't dare hope to see Dex lying there. If it turned out to be another person from town, Josh didn't think he could withstand the disappointment. But his throat tightened even more. And, as he rounded the horse and looked down at the man lying so still on the travois, the hot sting of tears burned in his nose and eyes.

"Dex," Josh gasped. He dropped to his knees beside the travois, hands hovering over him, afraid to touch Dex for fear of hurting him or, possibly worse, discover he was seeing things and it wasn't Dex at all.

Josh closed his eyes and asked, "It's him, right? It's Dex."

"It is," Glory replied, her voice soft.

Josh let out his breath and opened his eyes, looking down at Dex through his tears. The man lay strapped tight into the travois, his eyes closed, and his face covered with some kind of herbal mixture. Leaves had been affixed to his throat and shoulders with what appeared to be the same mixture, and the leaves continued below the blanket that covered him.

"Oh, Dex," Josh whispered. "You came home. You came back." He heard Glory speaking with the Indian brave above him as he looked Dex over. Placing a gentle hand on Dex's forehead, Josh felt the heat coming off him even through the herbal paste and leaves. He looked up at Glory and asked, "What's wrong with him? What are these leaves for?"

Glory nodded to the Indian as the man finished speaking, then met Josh's gaze. "He was badly sunburned when they found him. He had been walking through Venom Valley and fell in his tracks. He had to have been out there all day. They took him back to their camp, and he was fevered and talking wildly. They gave him medicine and applied the herbs and leaves which should speed the healing of his skin. The elders of the tribe did not want him there overnight, however, because they saw that he's been bitten. They feared Balthazar would take revenge on them for saving him, so they had these three bring him to town."

Josh's stomach clenched tight, and he could not draw a breath. Balthazar had bitten Dex. Fresh tears filled his eyes, and he angrily dried them on his shirtsleeve before getting to his feet and reaching for the nearest rope. The Indian helped Josh loosen the bindings that secured Dex within the travois, then he lifted Dex's feet and Josh grabbed beneath his arms. Unconscious, Dex was dead weight, but Josh could feel the warmth of his body and see his chest rise and fall with breath. Dex was alive. Whether or not he had been bitten, Dex was alive and had come home. Beatrice had been bitten and still lived as normal. Josh had to believe that Dex would as well. Dex would live, he had to.

Josh heard the words echoing over and over inside his head as he and the Indian carried Dex into the smithy. Dex would live. Dex would live. Dex would live.

"Is that Dex Wells?" Doc Brandt said. "Good Lord in heaven, what's happened to him?"

"Not sure," Josh said, and then looked at Glory. "Can you rouse Donegan? I want to put Dex on the bed."

Glory nodded and moved off into the darkness ahead of them. Josh heard Donegan snort and sputter then grouse a bit about being awakened, but when they rounded the corner of the low wall, the bed was empty and the sheets smoothed out. They lay Dex on the bed and the Indian stepped back, his dark eyes curious.

Josh peeled aside a few leaves to reveal Dex's chest, the dark chest hairs matted and tangled with the herbal paste. Beneath the mixture, Josh could see patches of sunburned skin and winced before reapplying the leaves. He lifted two leaves on the left side of his neck, exposing raw red wounds and bite marks. The sight made him light-headed. With trembling fingers, he replaced the leaves and leaned back. Right now, Dex needed rest, food, and water.

Josh stood, his sudden movement startling the Indian into taking two steps back. Josh nodded to him and held up his hand in a gesture for him to wait, then turned to Glory and said, "Help me?"

She approached to stand beside him. "How?"

"Help me tell him thank you," Josh said. "I want to say it myself, not just have you say it for me."

Glory spoke slowly, keeping her gaze on him as he cautiously repeated what she said, hoping he was pronouncing it correctly. It came out sounding like "Ahee-ih-yeh." After Josh said the words to him, the Indian smiled and nodded.

Then the Indian's smile slipped away, and he looked at Glory. Speaking quickly and using sharp hand movements, the man delivered a message that made Glory stiffen her spine and tighten her jaw. When the man finished speaking, Glory dipped her chin slightly in a nod and the brave walked back toward the doors.

"What did he say?" Josh asked Glory.

She took a moment to answer him, her jaw clenched and eyes narrowed with anger as she watched the young man's retreating back. "He told us the elders want us to keep out of their lands. They want no part in our fight with the demon nightwalker."

"But they've lost people to Balthazar as well," Josh said.

Glory looked at him, glanced down at Dex, and then back up at Josh. "He said Dex has been tainted by Balthazar. To them, he may as well be dead. When a member of the tribe is this close to turning, they kill him. The elders decided to let us have the honor of sending Dex on, to allow him to be buried in his own land."

"Dex will not die," Josh said, hearing the tremor in his own voice. "He's alive, and as long as he draws breath, he's still himself, still Dexter Wells." He looked around, panic building inside his chest, making it difficult for him to breathe. He wasn't going to lose Dex, not now when he'd just gotten him back. "Doc? Doc!"

Doc Brandt shuffled out of the shadows, licking his lips and wringing his hands. "I can look him over, Josh, but I don't know what more I can do for him."

"Just examine him, please," Josh said.

"I need more light," Doc grumbled as he knelt beside the bed.

Beatrice grabbed a lantern from across the smithy and dodged a kick from Sally as she crossed to stand at Dex's bedside. Outside, the Indians turned their horses back the way they had come and rode off down the street without looking back.

Josh waited a few minutes in silence, pacing, but finally had to ask, "How is he?"

Doc Brandt looked at him, and the expression on his face shattered something inside Josh's chest, something he had been holding delicately in place since Dex had been taken. Tears stung his eyes, but he pressed his lips together and kept them at bay. When he trusted his voice not to shake, Josh said, "He's not dead. I've seen him drawing breath. He's not dead."

"He's close," Brandt said, struggling to his feet. "He's lost a lot of blood, and he's been out in the sun with no food or water for a full day, maybe longer. Infection might set in, God knows what those Injuns smeared on his skin." His gaze flicked over Josh's shoulder to where Glory stood, and he cleared his throat and looked away as he mumbled, "No offense."

"The herbs will heal the sunburn quickly," Glory said, her voice cool. "He can replace the lost blood over time."

Doc Brandt grunted, but Josh knew the man didn't believe her. He didn't care. He just wanted Dex to open his eyes and talk to him.

"Yes, well, we still don't know what happened to him," Brandt grumbled. "There are puncture marks in his neck, I suppose that could explain the blood loss."

"How many?" Josh asked. He closed his eyes as he waited for the response. "How many marks?"

"Two sets, one on each side of his neck," Brandt told him, then shook his head. "If I didn't know better, I'd say they were bite marks, but I don't know what kind of animal has a bite like that."

"No animal," Josh said. "Vampire."

Doc Brandt grunted and looked away. "Whatever it was, it knew where to bite him. Looks like the bites were right over his carotid arteries. Surprised he lived through it." He snapped his gaze over to Josh, realized what he had said, then let out a breath as his shoulders sagged. "To properly care for him, I need to take him to my office."

"It's not safe," Josh said. "Once the sun goes down, we all

have to stay together. We've secured this building from the wolves, and none of the vampires have permission to enter."

"Vampires," Brandt said with a snort. "All right. I'll bring what I need down from my office. I'll need some help."

"I'll help," Glory offered.

"Me too," Beatrice said.

"Yes, that's fine. Come on."

Josh watched the three walk out the door, then he looked back down at Dex and let out a shaky breath. Across the smithy, Donegan was back at work hammering fire-softened silver into blades, each hammer strike like a blow against Josh's heart. He sat on the floor beside the bed and took Dex's hand, sticky with herbs and burning with fever. Out of sight of Donegan in his position, Josh placed a soft kiss on the back of Dex's hand, then used his sleeve to wipe the light smear of herbal paste from his lips.

"Come back to me, Dex," Josh said quietly. "You can't leave me here alone. We haven't had enough time together yet. Come back."

CHAPTER

NINETEEN

Just after sunset, the first of the vampires stood outside the smithy, shrieking up at the sky.

"They're in pain," Doc Brandt said as he stomped up to Josh. "For the love of God, shoot them!"

Josh shook his head. "Won't do any good, Doc. Bullets don't hurt 'em unless they're made of silver, and we've got too few of those to waste on target practice."

Doc Brandt's thick, white eyebrows drew down, and he glowered at Josh. "Can't you hear those people are suffering? If you won't put them out of their pain, I will. I can't stand by and listen to that screaming."

The doc grabbed up a rifle loaded with lead, not silver, and stalked to the door. Josh trotted after the man and pressed a palm against the door to keep him from opening it. "You can have your shot at them if you want, Doc, but only from the windows where we left spaces in the boards. You can't open the door."

"Damn fools," Doc muttered. He set himself up at the window, took aim, and fired off a couple of shots.

Josh stood watching the man's face for a reaction. He saw the doc's brows knit together again in a frown as he squinted out into the night.

"I could have sworn I hit 'em," Doc said in a low voice. "But they didn't even flinch."

"Probably did hit 'em," Josh assured him. "It just doesn't affect 'em."

A vampire pressed his face against the gap in the boards and shrieked at them. Everyone in the smithy screamed, and Doc Brandt took two startled steps back, then raised the rifle and shot the man in the face. The vampire vanished, and Doc Brandt turned to give Josh a victorious look before he stepped up to the window again.

"There, you see?" Doc Brandt said. "Just needed to actually hit one of 'em."

"Careful, Doc," Josh cautioned.

The vampire's face appeared again in the gap at the window, and he shrieked at them. From where he stood, Josh could see the black marks from the lead that had struck the man's face, but the skin was not broken.

"Can't be," Doc Brandt whispered.

"Only silver," Josh said, stepping up to the window. He grabbed one of the muskets loaded with a silver ball, aimed at the gap in the boards, and fired.

The vampire dropped to the dirt. Silence filled the smithy, feeling somehow louder than the vampire's shriek. Josh and Doc Brandt stepped cautiously up to the window and peered out to where the man lay still, a smoking black hole in his forehead.

"God help us," Doc Brandt whispered.

"Someone's got to," Josh said. He handed him the musket before turning to walk back toward the forge.

Donegan had his head down as he worked hard, muscular arms flexing in the lantern light. At the back of the smithy, Sally sat in a pile of hay with her legs curled under her, wrists secured. Josh was unnerved by the plotting he could see in her narrowed eyes as she sat there, her gaze watchful as a wicked barn cat on the prowl.

Josh knelt by Dex's side, listening to his deep, even breathing. After Doc Brandt had returned from his office, he had examined Dex more closely and discovered that his left thumb had been pulled out of joint and moved back into place. The skin around Dex's wrists was chafed and, in some places on the left, gouged deep and crusted with dried blood. The bite wounds on either side of Dex's neck were red and ragged, and a chill ball of anguish formed in Josh's gut. What the two bites meant, however, was beyond Josh. Beatrice had been bitten once and seemed to be all right other than a heightened sensitivity to sunlight. Josh just wished Dex would open his eyes and say something.

He stretched out on the floor beside Dex's bed, his back cushioned by a thin mat of straw. With his hands crossed over his chest, he let his gaze trace the seams between the boards in the ceiling. Now and then a howl or shriek from outside would startle everyone, and Doc Brandt or Donegan would let out a string of curses that made Beatrice giggle. After a time, Josh slipped into a light, uneasy sleep.

The long, dark night passed, the sounds of the wolves and the vampires in the street gnawing on everyone's nerves and waking Josh now and again from his fitful sleep. As if on schedule, a wolf would attack the doors or a boarded-up window at the top of each hour, startling everyone. They took turns with a long, sharpened stick that they poked through well-placed gaps to fend the beasts off.

When there was just an hour until sunrise, a voice whispered through the smithy, bringing them all to their feet.

"You took back what I stole from you," Balthazar said. "And here you are, still cowering inside your flimsy fortress, building weapons you hope will hurt me. But you have no power here. Let me in, let me take away Dex's pain and show the rest of you how much power awaits you."

"Yes!" Sally shouted. She strained against the chain holding her in place, hands before her, fingers reaching for the doors. "Take me, master! I am yours. I bid you to enter!"

"She cain't invite him in, can she?" Beatrice said, her voice high and tight with fear.

"She doesn't own this place," Josh assured her, hoping he was right. "Only Donegan can invite him in."

Donegan looked at Josh, eyes wide with terror. "I ain't invitin' him inside."

"Keep calm everyone," Josh said. "We're safe inside here."

"Take me, master!" Sally cried. "Let me walk beside you forever!"

"Get hold of yourself, woman!" Doc Brandt shouted at her. In the lantern's glow, his face was pale and his eyes wide with terror.

Then Balthazar whispered, "Dex."

Dex's eyes snapped open and he gasped. Josh dropped to his knees beside the bed, caught Dex's flailing right hand in his own as he placed a palm on Dex's forehead in an attempt to soothe him. But Dex wasn't ready to be soothed. He let out a shout of fear and shoved Josh away. He sat up and pressed his back against the half wall at the side of the bed, eyes wide with terror.

"Josh!" Glory shouted. She started toward him, but he held up a hand to keep her back.

Locking his gaze with Dex's, Josh spoke in a calm, quiet voice. "Dex, it's Josh. You're in Belkin's Pass. You're safe. You're home."

Dex's gaze darted away from Josh's face, back, away again, then back. A spark of recognition flickered into life, and Dex blinked rapidly as tears filled his eyes.

"Josh?" Dex whispered in a scratchy, ruined voice.

A sob choked Josh, burning the back of his throat, and his tears temporarily blinded him. He blotted his eyes with his sleeve and nodded. "It's me," he managed to say, then again, "It's me."

"Josh." This time his statement was filled with relief instead of a frightened question.

Josh moved to sit on the bed beside Dex, pulled him into his arms and clung to him. Tears streamed down his face, and he didn't care who in the smithy could see the depth of his emotion. The important thing was Dex was back and safe. Everything else they could learn to deal with.

"Sodomites?" Sally said, her disapproval evident in her tone.

"You have no room to judge," Glory said in response.

Something heavy slammed against the smithy doors, startling all of them, and Dex's fingers dug into Josh's back as the man moaned low in his throat.

"It's okay," Josh whispered. He pulled back from Dex but still gently held his hands, mindful of Dex's injured thumb. "We're safe."

Dex nodded and looked around. "Where are we?"

"The blacksmith shop."

Dex craned his neck to look over the knee wall at the

doors as they shook beneath another onslaught. "What is that?"

Josh shook his head. "Wolves, maybe. Or vampires turned by Balthazar. He's left them to run wild around the town."

"He's strong," Dex whispered as he turned back. "And smart. Smarter than we'd thought."

"What else do you remember?" Josh asked. "Anything that can help us?"

Dex shook his head slowly, his gaze becoming distant and frightened as he thought. "Screaming. And a cave."

The wood doors let out a sharp, popping crack as something attacked them again. Everyone jumped and gasped once more. Josh touched Dex's arm and whispered to him. "Stay here." He got to his feet and stood in front of the closed doors. Taking a deep breath, he prepared himself, clenching and releasing his fists.

"What are you doing?" Glory said. "You can't open those doors. The wolves will take you before you get a chance to shoot."

Josh shook his head. "I'm not opening them." He lifted his head, straightened his spine, and said in as strong and steady a voice as he could manage, "I know you can hear me, Balthazar. Leave this place. Leave us, or die."

A heavy blow sounded against the doors in response, and then Balthazar's voice slithered through the smithy. The horses snorted and stomped, and from the corner of his eye, Josh saw Beatrice shudder and cross her arms.

"You may have some limited power over the stupid, stumbling dead made of rotting flesh with no thoughts of their own, but you do not know what true power is, Josh

Stanton. I can command those I've sired when I want. Behold."

Silence fell, sudden and deafening. Josh held his breath, gaze flicking from the doors to the boarded windows and back. Finally, he let out his breath and stepped to a window. He hesitated, then leaned closer to peer through the small crack between the boards.

The townspeople Balthazar had turned stood in rows before the smithy, hands at their sides, the white light of the quarter moon glinting off the points of their fangs. Wolves sat in a line behind the vampires, tongues hanging out, and eyes glittering in the moonlight.

"He controls them?" Doc Brandt asked in a quiet voice from where he peered out the window on the other side of the doors.

Josh turned away from the window and looked at each of them in turn. "We still have the upper hand. We know what kills them. And the last couple of days, we've been killing them during the day as we search the town, so there are fewer out there now."

The doors shuddered, and the wood around the hinges splintered. Josh stepped back, heart pounding, fingertips tingling as he stared at the doors, watched as they leaned in. Another assault, and the wood in the frame gave, the nails shrieking as they pulled free. A cloud of dust and straw blew over Josh as the doors fell flat onto the floor of the smithy. Everyone shouted in terror and scrambled back.

Josh stood his ground. He reached up to touch Dex's gold cross that hung around his neck. The vampires stood outside the door, eyes glowing red, fangs bared. The wolves stood just behind them, lips pulled up in snarls.

"You have no cover," Balthazar said, his voice a sinister whisper that felt like snake scales across Josh's skin. He floated down from above the door to stand in front of his cursed children.

"God in heaven," Doc Brandt whispered. "He flies?"

Balthazar fixed the doc with a look, and Josh shouted, "Don't look at him!"

"Take me, master!" Sally shouted. "Let me live forever beside you."

Balthazar ignored Sally as he turned his gaze on Josh. "You are helpless against us. With a flick of my finger—" Balthazar moved an index finger, and a wolf stepped between two vampires to rush the doors. Josh reached out as it leaped at him, grabbed handfuls of fur on either side of its neck as the weight of it forced him to fall on his back. The wolf's slobber spattered across his face, and the beast's breath washed over him, hot and rank as its jaws snapped an inch above his nose.

A gunshot exploded behind him. The wolf jumped in his grip and blood splashed hot across Josh's face as the animal sagged heavy and dead on top of him. He pushed it aside and sat up. Looking over his shoulder, he saw Glory holding a rifle. They nodded to each other and Josh got to his feet, wiping the blood from his face and glaring at Balthazar.

"You cannot get to us."

"So be it," Balthazar said, one corner of his lip curled up in a sneer that revealed the fang on that side. "You'll beg me to turn you when the wolves have their muzzles buried in your guts."

Another gunshot from behind Josh made him drop to a crouch. A splash of dark blood exploded on Balthazar's right shoulder, and the vampire shrieked in pain. Josh looked behind him to where Donegan held a smoking muzzleloader, one of the guns they had loaded with a silver ball. The black-smith's expression was a mix of fear and determination as he said in a loud, strong voice, "You are refused entrance here. Leave this place."

Balthazar snarled at Donegan, his left hand clamped over his right shoulder as he shouted, "Kill!" Then he turned and, in a blink, was gone from sight.

The wolves leaped through the doors, snarling and snapping.

CHAPTER

TWENTY

Ohanzee's presence strengthened around her, and Glory went against her natural instincts, relaxing her muscles to allow him to guide her movements. She dodged two wolves, moving right and left until she reached their stash of weapons. Taking up a long, silver blade, she gripped the handle tight and felt Ohanzee spin her as she brought the sword up to decapitate both wolves in one swing.

A scream caught her attention, and she turned to see Beatrice on her back on the floor, punching and kicking as three wolves bit and clawed at her. Glory moved fast, slashing and stabbing with her sword until the two biting Beatrice's legs were dead. Beatrice grabbed the wolf standing on her chest by the neck, then drove the short knife she wielded deep into its throat. Blood splashed down onto Beatrice's chest, and the wolf sagged in her grip before she pulled out the knife and pushed the body aside.

"Can you walk?" Glory asked, standing before Beatrice with her sword ready.

"Don't know," Beatrice moaned. "They bit deep."

"Doc!" Glory shouted. "We need you!" She looked around the smithy, picking out the wolves. At least ten remained. As she watched, one of the farmers from just outside town, one of only two who had returned that night to the smithy, ran to the doors seeking escape, two wolves snapping at his heels. Before Glory could shout a warning, the man was grabbed by a vampire waiting just over the threshold and dragged screaming to the ground. The rest of the vampires fell on him, and the wolves that had been chasing him turned back toward the room.

"Help!"

Glory looked toward the corner where Dex had been resting, and saw Doc Brandt swinging a board at two wolves. The creatures had Dex and the doctor cornered. The wolves slowly advanced, snapping at the board in the doctor's hands.

"Stay here," Glory said to Beatrice. She ran across the room, ducking and dodging, slashing and stabbing as she went. Sally stood with her back pressed against the wall to which she was chained, her eyes wide and hair a wild mess as she laughed and watched the wolves chase the rest of them. None of the wolves approached Sally, and Glory knew Balthazar was protecting her.

Glory killed the wolves threatening Dex and the doc and spun around. Only five wolves remained, one attacking Donegan, which Beatrice limped up behind and stabbed in the hip as Glory watched. Two others had Josh cornered, but before she could move, someone grabbed the sword from her hand.

Dex took her sword and ran across the room, the leaves

applied by the Indian tribe fluttering off his sunburned skin as he went. He cut down the wolves then fell to his knees and let the sword clatter to the floor. Josh knelt beside him and put his arm around Dex's shoulders, whispering to him. Dex's bandaged hand shook, and blood seeped through the wrappings.

The other two wolves retreated to the doors, lips pulled back and tails tucked. Once they had crossed the threshold, they turned and ran off into the night, and Glory felt Ohanzee's presence fading. Doc Brandt stood beside her, but his attention was fixed on the vampires outside the doors as they tore and drank from the body. Glory heard Ohanzee say, "Josh stones," and then he was gone.

Doc Brandt dragged a shaking hand across his brow and turned to look at her. "What kind of devils are they?"

"Vampires," Glory stated. "We've told you, now you see for yourself."

"Dear God in heaven, is that what became of my wife and daughter?" Doc Brandt said.

Glory didn't know how to respond, so she kept silent. Sobbing caught her attention and she looked around. She gasped and grabbed the doc's arm, pulling him along as she hurried over to Beatrice. The bites on Beatrice's leg were bleeding badly, but Beatrice wasn't attending to her injuries. Instead, she lay with her ear pressed against Donegan's chest.

"I think he's dead," Beatrice said. "I cain't hear his heart."

"Move aside," Doc Brandt said. Glory pulled Beatrice back to rest against her as the doc looked at the wounds in Donegan's shoulder and throat.

"Your leg, Bea," Glory said. "Let me tend to it."

Beatrice sniffled and nodded. Glory got up to fetch a

bowl of clean water and some bandages from the bed area. As she crossed back to Beatrice, she heard Sally giggling.

"Shut your foul mouth, Sally, or I'll cut out your tongue," Glory said.

Sally glared at her but quieted. Glory returned to kneel by Beatrice and dabbed at the bites. Beatrice flinched, but kept her gaze on Donegan, and Glory understood that while they had all been trying to figure out how to stay alive, Beatrice had grown fond of Donegan.

Doc sat back and shook his head. "I'm sorry, he's gone."

"No," Beatrice said quietly, then louder, "No! He's a good man! It ain't fair!"

"What?" Josh said from just behind Glory. "Donegan is dead?"

Glory looked up at him and saw that his face had paled. She realized suddenly the effect Donegan's body would have on him. She stood up, her stomach tight with tension. "Will you be okay?"

Josh looked frightened and sweat stood out on his forehead, but he nodded. "Yes. I'm sorry, Beatrice. He was a good man, and we all will miss him." Josh met Glory's gaze once more, then turned to where Dex stood beside him and said, "I need to sit as far from him as I can get."

Dex nodded and together they moved to the front corner of the smithy.

Doc Brandt frowned toward Dex and Josh then looked at Glory. He appeared to want to say something but stopped when a sudden movement outside the door caught their attention. A number of vampires crouched just outside the threshold of the door, feeding on the body of the unfortunate farmer who had been fleeing the wolves. They all stood at the same moment and turned to look east, blood staining their faces and their eyes glowing red.

"Sunrise soon," Glory said.

One moment the vampires stood outside the door, and the next they were gone, returning to wherever they had found to lie during the day.

"My Lord," Doc Brandt whispered. "That fast?"

"That fast," Glory assured him. "Can you tend to Beatrice's leg?"

"What? Oh, yes. Of course." Doc took the bandages from her and moved to kneel beside Beatrice.

"Glory, don't leave me," Beatrice said, her face streaked with tears.

"Not far," Glory assured her. "Within sight."

Glory crossed the room to kneel beside Josh and touch his arm. "Are you controlling it?"

Josh looked at her, his expression pained. "Barely. Still too close to the body."

"I may have something that can help you." Glory reached inside her shirt and produced the small bag of crystals.

"What's that?" Dex asked.

Glory opened the top of the drawstring bag and tipped it to allow the different colored stones to tumble into her palm. The lantern light glittered along the surface of each stone, and Glory felt the power of the crystals hum through her body.

"These are crystals," Glory explained. "Sacred to my people. They help with many types of energy and provide protection. I believe we can find one to help you focus the power inside you."

Josh nodded. "I'll try anything."

"When the sun's up, we'll move the body," Dex said.

"When the sun's up, you'll be getting a bath," Josh replied, and the two men shared a look that made Glory blush and look away.

"Come to me when you're ready," Glory said, then rose and walked to the doors to watch the sky lighten.

TWENTY-ONE

The water was hot, and Dex hissed as he lowered himself into the tub. He and Josh had come to the One-Eyed Rooster and found the tin tub in Sally's private room as Glory had promised. As Dex had slowly undressed and removed his bandages, Josh walked up and down the steps with pails of water from the well out back, heating half of them on a fire in the hearth, until the tub was almost full.

"The water's already dirty," Josh said as Dex settled back in the tub. "That explains the smell coming off you."

Dex narrowed his eyes. "You spend days in a cave and then wander around Venom Valley and see how you smell."

"My apologies." Josh dipped a cloth in the water and rubbed it with a bar of Sally's lavender scented soap to create a fine smelling lather. "Tell me if it hurts," Josh said, moving it in gentle circles across Dex's shoulders.

"Feels good," Dex assured him, and it did. Josh's touch got him hard, and he pulled his knees up to hide his condition. He ached for Josh, but now didn't feel like the right time.

"Sunburn's faded quite a bit already," Josh noted. "Those leaves and whatever else the Indians covered you with helped."

"It feels better," Dex said. "Now I'm just... tired."

"Doc says that's the loss of blood," Josh explained. He carefully touched a corner of the cloth to the one of the bite marks on Dex's neck, apologizing when Dex flinched.

"Stings," Dex said. He shuddered at the sudden memory of Balthazar lowering his mouth to his neck and the popping sound of his fangs breaking through skin, wet and sharp in his ear.

They were quiet a long time as Josh washed him. When he circled the tub to be able to reach his other side, Dex ran the soap over his legs. So much lay unspoken between them, so much that Dex had no clear memory of. He remembered the sound of screaming, but not the screamer's identity. For all he knew, it could have been his own. He remembered feeling anger and jealousy for Josh, but he wasn't clear why. To help himself focus, Dex closed his eyes and lowered his head, letting his mind drift while Josh scrubbed him clean of dirt and dried blood.

"I'm wet," Josh said, his voice bringing Dex back from a memory of seeing Venom Valley stretched out before him, shimmering in the sunlight and his throat dry as rock. Dex blinked and looked up, hardening once again as he watched Josh remove his shirt that had been splashed with water. The gold cross around his neck caught the sun and Dex reached up, his fingers hesitating a moment. Was he unclean? Could he still touch his cross or would it burn him? He closed his eyes and stretched out his hand, feeling the smooth surface of the cross beneath his fingertips. A slight tingle ran up his arm, but there was no pain, and he let out a relieved breath.

"Do you remember giving that to me?" Josh asked.

Dex nodded, keeping his gaze on the cross. "I do. And I remember lying with you at the Indian camp."

"Yes." Josh sounded relieved. "It's one of my favorite memories." Emboldened by Josh's tone, Dex pushed himself to his feet and stood in the tub. His cock stood out hard and proud, pointing at Josh as if to claim him.

"Oh, Dex," Josh said, reaching down to take hold of him.

Dex closed his eyes and let out a shaky breath. "I thought I'd never feel you touch me again." He remembered suddenly the cold feel and dry taste of Balthazar's cock, and he flinched. More memories spun into his mind after that. Horrible memories. Icy come pulsing into his mouth and down his throat. Each of the bites Balthazar had delivered on Dex's neck. He closed his eyes and shivered.

"You're shivering. Does it hurt?" Josh asked, releasing him.

Dex shook his head and looked at him with tears in his eyes. How could he tell Josh what had happened and make him understand how little control he had really had? "No, it doesn't hurt. I'm just remembering more of... it."

"Oh." Josh looked away, then back again. "Did he...?" Josh looked down at Dex's cock, still held in his hand and back up into his face, leaving the question unasked.

Dex nodded. "Once. He had me take him in my mouth. I can still taste his cold flesh and his...." He stopped and clenched his fists before forcing himself to continue, practically spitting out the words as his cock softened in Josh's grip. "I swallowed his spoiled seed." Shame and anger collided within his chest, and he stepped from the tub, slinging dirty water and scented suds across the fine rug.

"Dex, wait!"

Josh's voice brought him to a stop. Dex stood with his back to Josh, nude and dripping on the rug with his fists clenched, the left still impossible to tighten fully because of his swollen thumb. How long until he could hold a gun again? Until he could protect Josh and the others?

"I'm unclean," Dex whispered, head lowered, eyes squeezed shut. "Tainted by him."

"You are still the man I grew up loving." Josh squeezed his shoulders gently, and Dex felt the warm touch of Josh's chest against his back. Soft kisses swept across the skin of his shoulders and Dex let out a long, shuddering breath. Something that had been clenched tight inside his chest suddenly released.

"Truth?" Dex asked in a quiet, shaky voice. It was what they used to say when they were young and something the other had said surprised them.

Josh let out a quiet, sad laugh. "Truth."

He was home. Josh was here and still loved him. All would be right if he could just hold to that truth.

Dex turned quick, caught Josh's mouth with his own and put his arms around him. Dex's cock surged again, feeling like stone pressed against Josh's thigh, and they moaned in unison as their tongues rolled together.

"Missed you," Josh managed to say.

Dex fumbled to open Josh's trousers, his left hand slow and stiff. Josh finally reached down to do it for him, letting them fall to the floor. Dex knelt and pulled down Josh's drawers, catching the fat tip of his cock between his lips as it bobbed before him. The taste of Josh's fevered skin burst across his tongue, salty and delicious, and Dex moaned as he took Josh deep into his throat.

"Oh, Dex," Josh said with a sigh, curling his fingers in his wet hair.

Dex sucked him hard and fast, eager for his semen, wanting the taste of Josh to banish the lingering reminder of Balthazar. He took hold of Josh's balls and pulled, then lifted his right hand and pinched a nipple. In moments, Josh grunted, and hot, thick come flooded Dex's mouth. The sharp tang of it tasted like cool water on a summer day, and he swallowed it eagerly, felt the warmth spread out from the center of his belly.

Josh reached down to pull him to his feet for a kiss. "You were hungry."

"I still am," Dex said, and took his hand. "I need more of you."

Josh stepped out of his clothes and let Dex led him to Sally's bed, Josh's cock twitching and lengthening as he walked. Dex lay on his back and lifted his legs as he met Josh's gaze. "I want you inside me."

"You're sure?" Josh said as clear fluid dribbled from Dex's cock to puddle on his belly. "We've never done that."

"More sure than about anything else," Dex assured him. "Please. I need this."

Josh looked around, then walked to the tub to grab the soap. He slicked himself with it and slid slippery fingers into Dex. The invasion felt good, and Dex was impatient to feel Josh push into him, take control of him, and fill him with the hot, sticky seed Dex craved. He needed Josh to stake a claim on him, mark him as his own.

"That's enough," Dex said, trying to keep the impatience out of his voice. "Take me."

Josh laughed, the sound so foreign it made them both smile.

"Been a long time since I laughed," Josh admitted.

Dex pulled him down for a rough kiss. "I'm glad I could be the cause of it. Now fuck me, Josh Stanton."

He felt the touch of Josh's cock at his threshold, then the sting of his entry. Dex moaned and closed his eyes, only to open them a moment later when Josh pulled back. "Don't stop," Dex said. "I want it. I need it. We need it."

Josh nodded, adjusted his stance, and then pushed into him again. Dex felt his muscles shift and stretch to make way as Josh's cock slowly, steadily filled him. When Josh was finally fully seated inside him, he leaned down for a kiss before easing out and back in again, then again.

"Feels so good," Josh said. "Your body holds to me like you don't want me to leave."

"I don't," Dex said, pulling him down for another kiss. "Ever."

"Never," Josh assured him, the gold cross dangling between them. He straightened up and took hold of Dex's ankles. Slowly at first, Josh pumped his hips, making sure Dex was okay. In short time, he hammered at Dex's hole, thrusting hard and deep.

"Close," Dex almost shouted. A breeze blew across him from a broken window, and Dex's sweat cooled. He reached down to stroke himself as Josh quickened his pace even more. All Dex knew was the feeling of Josh inside him, deep within him where no one else had touched him before. It would be Josh's seed he held inside himself afterward, Josh's come that would remove the stain of Balthazar from his body for good.

"I love you," Josh whispered and reached down to take hold of Dex's cock at the root as he plunged into him a final time. "I'm coming."

Dex shouted Josh's name as the rush of climax swept through him as well. Semen landed on his face and coated his belly. He felt the pulse of Josh's cock within him, filling him, healing him. They panted together afterwards, catching their breath. Then Josh gave him a soft, simple kiss on the lips before easing out of him. He slid a single finger inside to push his leavings back into Dex.

Slowly Dex lowered his legs and sat up. He put his arms around Josh's waist and pressed a kiss to the smooth, sweaty skin of his belly. The warm, sweat-sticky feel of Josh's skin felt good after the days of cold touches and damp, rough stone.

"Now we both need a bath," Josh said.

Dex smiled up at him. "Easier to share a tub."

Josh smiled back. "You drain the water and I'll fetch clean."

They kissed and Josh pulled on his trousers as Dex unstoppered the drain in the bottom of the tub. He listened to the water rush through the copper pipe that stuck out over the back of the Rooster where it would drain into the dirt, splattering mud on anyone within three feet. Only Sally would have had such a convenience.

Some time later, they sat facing each other in the water, taking turns with the soap. Dex let Josh inspect the wounds around his wrists and his bruised and swollen thumb.

"Doc says it'll heal," Josh said. "But it might affect your shooting."

Dex nodded. "Good thing I can shoot with both hands."

"Good thing." Josh placed a gentle kiss on his thumb and then on each raw, chafed wrist before sitting back against the side of the tub. "Do you remember anything about the location of the cave?"

Dex let out a breath and closed his eyes, trying to remember more. "I know it was close to the end of Venom Valley, where the narrow passage leads to the open prairie." He shook his head, struggling. Cave walls, screams, and the rattle of chains. But just before he opened his eyes, a memory snapped into focus. The screaming in the cave had come from a woman, and he could see her clearly. His heart pounded, and he sucked in a breath as he understood what he had seen. Dex opened his eyes and looked at Josh with such emotion the man sat up straight in his end of the tub.

"What is it?" Josh asked. "What did you remember?"

"We have to go there," Dex said. "We need to find his cave."

"Would it be safer to wait for him to come back to us?" Josh asked. "Donegan wounded him with a silver bullet, so we know for sure that could kill him."

Dex shook his head. "It's more than just him we have to go back for. He's got another prisoner."

Josh frowned. "Another prisoner? Who?"

Dex leaned forward to take Josh's hands. He winced at the pain in his thumb, but tightened his fingers when Josh tried to pull away. "Josh, I think he's got your mother. He's been holding her in that cave all these years."

CHAPTER
TWENTY-TWO

Josh leaned the last two muzzleloaders against the back wall of the church and looked across the pews to the pulpit at the front. Sally stood on the raised platform, shackled arms chained to the wall beneath the stained glass window. Her hair hung in clotted strands around her shoulders, and her pale skin gleamed in the lantern light. Josh didn't like having her in their midst, but it was better to keep her where they could see her than leave her free to plot against them. She had also overheard too much of their plans to let her go free and most likely tell Balthazar all she had learned.

He leaned out of the church doors, looking up and down the street. Beatrice and Dex approached from the blacksmith's, each wearing a hat to keep the setting sun off them, their arms filled with a variety of weapons. Two buttons of Dex's shirt had come open, and Josh could see the sunlight glint off the small key hanging around his neck. Josh had discovered it in the pocket of Dex's tattered and filthy trousers before he had discarded them, and when he had shown it to Dex, the man had closed it in his fist without a word. After their shared bath, Dex had found a thin chain in Sally's jewelry box and hung the key around his neck. When Josh asked him what it opened, Dex said simply, "My heart," and left it at that.

Josh noticed that Beatrice limped from the wolf bites on her leg, and that she kept her gaze cast down to the ground. Donegan's death had really affected Beatrice. She was quiet now, withdrawn, and Josh worried about her. They were each going to need to be stronger and braver than ever before to take on Balthazar out in Venom Valley.

And to set Josh's mother free.

He turned his mind away from any consideration of what Balthazar had put her through over the last fifteen years. From the little Dex had been able to tell him, she had lost her mind and could only sit in her stone prison and wail.

Anger laced with hatred churned within him, bitter and hot, but Josh closed his eyes and pushed it away. He needed to keep his thoughts calm and focused if they were to defeat Balthazar once and for all. There were only five of them now: Doc Brandt, Glory, Dex, Beatrice, and himself. Five of them against Balthazar and his battalion of vampires and wolves.

"Josh?" Glory stood beside him, startling him.

"I didn't hear you," Josh said.

"Do you have time before sunset?" Glory asked. She held out her hand to display the different colored stones. "I think we should try."

Josh frowned. "How?"

"With Donegan."

Josh swallowed past a hard lump. "Glory, I don't know. It

doesn't seem right. It's such a... an invasion. You just don't understand."

"It may be our only chance against him," Glory said. "And it would be a way to avenge Donegan's death."

Josh took a breath and squinted at the sun hanging low in the sky. They should have an hour of daylight left. He looked at her and nodded. "All right. Let's go."

Doc Brandt and Dex had carried Donegan's body to the undertaker's and laid him out in the back room. When they had returned, Dex's face had been pale, and he said to Josh out of earshot of the others, "There were so many bodies back there. Torn apart, like they did to the farmer last night."

Josh felt the now familiar heat start up inside him as they climbed the steps to the undertaker's door. He paused and looked at Glory, his throat dry. "I feel them back there."

"I'll stay with you, don't worry. Here, try this one." She handed him a clouded green stone, and he gripped it in his fist.

"What do I do with it?"

"Focus your thoughts. If it doesn't help you direct them, we'll try a different one."

Josh nodded, took a breath, then opened the door and stepped inside the outer office. The smell pushed against them like a physical barrier, and both turned away to gasp. With watering eyes and the heat growing inside him, Josh turned to face the door to the back room, tightening his fingers around the stone. He couldn't go any closer. There were too many of them. All of them greedily drew energy from him.

He closed his eyes and pushed out his thoughts. He could feel them lying there, some missing limbs but willing to move however possible. The feeling, however, was the same as before—scattered, wild, unfocused—and he dropped the stone into Glory's palm.

"It's no different," he said. Sweat ran down his face, and his chest felt as if a glowing piece of coal from Donegan's forge was lodged there. He wanted to turn and run out to the street, escape the power blazing inside him and the stench of death around them.

Glory pressed a stone into his hand. "A new one."

Josh focused again, but felt the same. He handed it back, his palm sweating so much the stone clung to his skin. He accepted the next stone and tried once more with the same results. They went through four more stones with no luck and Josh felt exhaustion creeping in. It was no use. The crystals were just stones; there was no magic within them to help him harness his power. He was on the verge of telling Glory it was hopeless when she handed him a stone that shot a tingle up his arm.

His body stiffened, and he felt the power within him shift. It was as if the stone was a the lock on a door that finally slid home. Before, the power had felt feral, barely contained, something that happened to him without his consent. Now, it seemed to be harnessed to him instead of loose inside him. With his sharpened focus, he could feel the detailed structure of the bodies in the back room, the limits and possibilities of each one, and it did not tax him as it had before.

"This is it," Josh said and opened his eyes to look at Glory. He no longer felt overheated, no longer felt terrified of this power. It lived within him but didn't rule him. "My God, it really helps. What is it?"

"Carnelian," Glory said with a nod. "It increases magical powers."

Josh looked at the orange stone in his hand and then back at Glory. "It's amazing. I can feel them back there, but I'm keeping them in place without effort. It's like they're waiting for me to tell them what to do, and I don't have to think it to them like before." He took a breath, let it out. "Thank you."

"You are welcome," Glory said. "I'm glad we found a stone that works for you."

The sound of horses and a carriage in the street took them out to the boardwalk. Josh closed the undertaker's door behind them, and the feeling of the bodies in the back room faded away. He pocketed the crystal and followed Glory into the street where a carriage waited outside the blacksmith's shop. Two men in Army uniforms sat on top. When they saw them, they called to someone out of sight.

Sergeant Walker Maxwell stepped out of Donegan's shop and looked their way. At the sight of them, he smiled and Josh felt a nervous twist in his gut at how it transformed the man's face, made him even more handsome. Guilt reared up inside him as he thought about Dex and the intimacy they had so recently shared. Josh loved Dex. He didn't need to notice how handsome Walker Maxwell was. He furrowed his brow as he pushed those thoughts aside.

"Thought we'd lost you," Walker said as he approached, jerking a thumb over his shoulder at the smithy.

"We were attacked," Josh explained. "We lost some people, including Donegan."

Walker made a face. "The blacksmith?"

"Yes," Josh said. "Wolves got him. But our town doctor is back, and so is our deputy, Dexter Wells."

"Yeah? That's good news." Walker nodded to the wagon. "This was the only functional wagon left by the time I got back to the fort." He shook his head. "Just five men remained. The rest had taken off." He looked back at them, his face grim. "Most likely vampires."

"How many gone?" Glory asked.

Walker looked up at the sky as he thought. "Fifty maybe."

"Good God," Josh said as his stomach dropped. "All with military experience."

Walker nodded. "We'll need a good plan."

Josh nodded as well, then looked up at him in surprise. "We?"

"Yes we," Walker said. "Think I'm going to leave you all alone to go up against that? Besides, most of them are my men and therefore my responsibility."

"We should get inside," Glory suggested. "It will be dark soon."

Josh turned to point. "We're in the church. It's the safest."

"I'll pull the wagon around behind it. What about the horses?" Walker asked.

"We brought ours inside."

Walked made a face. "Into the church? Is that... proper?"

Josh looked at him. "It is when the town pastor is a vampire and packs of wolves are killing everything in sight."

"I see your point."

Josh watched him walk back toward the carriage, then continued on toward the church with Glory beside him.

"Fifty more vampires is a lot," Glory said.

"It is," Josh replied. "But I have a plan."

"What is it?" Glory asked.

"Let's gather everyone together and talk about it after the sun goes down," Josh said. "And we're going to need shovels. A lot of shovels."

"Shovels?" Glory frowned at him as they climbed the steps to the front doors of the church. Down the street, Walker turned the horses around and drove the wagon toward them.

"Who's that?" Dex asked, coming up to stand beside Josh.

"Sergeant Walker Maxwell," Josh said. "One of five remaining Army men from Fort Emmerick."

Dex seemed to stiffen beside him before he said, "Only five?"

Josh nodded. "That's it."

They watched the carriage turn and pass alongside the church and out of sight.

"Why do we need shovels?" Glory asked again.

Josh looked at her and then at Dex, his fingers finding and gripping the carnelian stone in his pocket. "To assemble an army of our own."

To be concluded in
BLOOD & STONE: VENOM VALLEY BOOK THREE

BLOOD & STONE: VENOM VALLEY BOOK THREE

Josh, Dex, and Glory return to continue their fight against Balthazar in the exciting final book of the Venom Valley Series:

A small mining town, lost.
New lovers fighting for their future.
An Army sergeant with secrets of his own.

With Belkin's Pass overrun by vampires and wolves, Josh Stanton, his lover, Dex, former saloon girl Glory, and US Army Sergeant Walker Maxwell, are forced to flee to the abandoned Fort Emmerick. There, they make plans to take the battle to Balthazar's cave in order to stop his plot to turn every human into a vampire.

But much stands in their way. Josh must learn to control his ability to raise the dead. The few survivors need to be trained to fight. And they will need a greater number of soldiers in order to triumph over Balthazar and the people he has turned. Their final, desperate battle will soon take place across the unforgiving landscape of Venom Valley, and the outcome will decide the fate of the entire country.

Grab your copy today: https://books2read.com/ bloodandstone

About the Author

Hank Edwards (he/him) has been writing gay fiction for more than twenty years. He has published over forty novels and novellas and dozens of short stories. His writing crosses many sub-genres, including contemporary romance, rom-com, paranormal, suspense, mystery, wacky comedy, and erotica. He has written a number of series such as the funny and spooky Critter Catchers, Old West historical horror of Venom Valley, suspenseful FBI and civilian Up to Trouble, and the erotic and funny Fluffers, Inc. Under the pen name R. G. Thomas, he has written a young adult urban fantasy gay romance series called The Town of Superstition. He was born and still lives in a northwest suburb of the Motor City, Detroit, Michigan.

For more information:
www.hankedwardsbooks.com
hankedwardsbooks@gmail.com
www.facebook.com/groups/hankshangout

ALSO BY HANK EDWARDS

Critter Catchers Series

Terror by Moonlight

Chasing the Chupacabra

Swamped by Fear

The Devil of Pinesville

Screams of the Season

Horror at Hideaway Cove

Dread of Night

Critter Catchers Box Set 1

Critter Catchers Box Set 2

Critter Catchers Universe Stories

The Mystery of the Morelock Motel

Critter Catchers: Level Up Series

Grave Danger

Wet Screams

Williamsville Inn Gay Romance:

Snowflakes and Song Lyrics

The Cupid Crawl

Fake Date Flip-Flop

Star-Spangled Showdown

Lacetown Murder Mysteries
(co-written with Deanna Wadsworth)

Murder Most Lovely

Murder Most Deserving

Venom Valley Series

Cowboys & Vampires

Stakes & Spurs

Blood & Stone

Up to Trouble Series

Holed Up

Shacked Up

Roughed Up

Choked Up

Fluffers, Inc. Series

Fluffers, Inc.

A Carnal Cruise

Vancouver Nights

Standalone Gay Romance

Buried Secrets

Destiny's Bastard

Hired Muscle

Plus Ones

Repossession is 9/10ths of the Law

Wicked Reflection

<u>Holiday Gay Romance:</u>

A Gift for Greg (A Story Orgy Single)

Mistletoe at Midnight (A Story Orgy Single)

The Christmas Accomplice

<u>Story Orgy Singles Gay Romance</u>:

A Gift for Greg

By the Book

Cross Country Foreplay

Mistletoe at Midnight

The Cheapskate: Bad Boyfriends

With This Ring

The Story Orgy Singles Boxed Set

<u>The Town of Superstition (YA urban fantasy series)</u>
<u>Published under pen name R. G. Thomas</u>

The Midnight Gardener

The Well of Tears

The Battle of Iron Gulch

A Tangle of Secrets

<u>Gay Erotic Short Story Collections</u>:

A Very Dirty Dozen

Another Very Dirty Dozen

A Third Very Dirty Dozen

A Fourth Very Dirty Dozen

<u>Salacious Singles Gay Erotic Short Stories</u>:

Bear Market

Convoy

Double Down

Exchange Rate

Finding North

Hotel Dick

Kindred Spirits

Sacked

Stroking Midnight

Vanity Loves Company

Wet Lands

www.ingramcontent.com/pod-product-compliance
Lightning Source LLC
Chambersburg PA
CBHW021959120726
47992CB00001B/324